SOMETHING, MAYBE

Also by Elizabeth Scott

Bloom
Perfect You
Living Dead Girl

SOMETHING, MAYBE

ELIZABETH SCOTT

Simon Pulse
New York London Toronto Sydney

SIMON PULSE
An imprint of Simon & Schuster Children's Publishing Division
1230 Avenue of the Americas, New York, NY 10020
Copyright © 2009 by Elizabeth Spencer
All rights reserved, including the right
of reproduction in whole or in part in any form.
SIMON PULSE and colophon are registered trademarks
of Simon & Schuster, Inc.
Designed by Tom Daly
The text of this book was set in Berkeley.
Manufactured in the United States of America
First Simon Pulse hardcover edition March 2009
2 4 6 8 10 9 7 5 3 1
Library of Congress Control Number 2008925771
ISBN-13: 978-1-4169-7865-7
ISBN-10: 1-4169-7865-8

Thanks to Jennifer Klonsky and everyone at Simon Pulse for all they do, and to Robin Rue for her support and kindness.

Thanks also to the usual suspects for reading drafts and providing encouragement, especially Clara Jaeckel and Donna Randa-Gomez.

This book never would have happened without Jessica Brearton—Jess, you wanted to read this story when all I had was a title and about two sentences, and thank you so much for encouraging me and reading it when you barely even had time to sleep! I owe you—well, I owe you a million for this one. And everything else.

one

Everyone's seen my mother naked.

Well, mostly naked. Remember that ad that ran during the Super Bowl, the one where a guy calls and orders a pizza and opens the door to see a naked lady with an open pizza box ("The pizza that's so hot it can't be contained!") covering the bits you still aren't allowed to see on network television?

That was her. Candy Madison, once one of Jackson James' girlfriends, and star of the short-lived sitcom *Cowboy Dad*. Now she's reduced to the (very rare) acting job or ad, but she was relatively famous (or infamous) for a few days after the football game with a pre-game show that lasts longer than the actual game.

Whoo.

You might think the ad caused me nothing but grief at

school, but aside from a few snide comments from the sparkly girls (you know the type: unnaturally white teeth, shining hair, personalities of rabid dogs) and some of the jock jerks (who, of course, were watching the game, and like both pizza and naked women—not a stretch to figure they'd be interested), no one else said anything to me.

But then, no one really talks to me. That's good, though. I've worked long and hard to be invisible at Slaterville High, an anonymous student in the almost 2,000 that attend, and I want it to stay that way. (The school website actually boasts that we're larger than some colleges. I guess overcrowding is a good thing now.)

However, the ad has caused me nothing but grief at home. When it aired, traffic to Mom's site, candymadison.net, tripled, and she worked to keep it coming back, giving free "chats" (where she sits around in lingerie and answers questions about her so-called career and Jackson), and pushing her self-published autobiography, *Candy Madison: Taking It All Off.* We actually sold ten of the twenty-five cases of the thing stacked in our garage.

And the press coverage? Mom loved it. The ad only ran once, because some senator's kid saw it and . . . you know where I'm going, right?

Of course you do, and naturally, the ad became extremely popular online. *Celeb Weekly* magazine did five questions with her, and Mom pushed her website and book and then talked about how she was always looking for "interesting, quirky character roles."

The week it ran, Mom bought ten copies of the magazine at

the grocery store and wandered around the house grinning and flapping the interview at me. The phone rang almost hourly, her brand-new agent calling with offers (mostly for work involving no clothing, which Mom turned down) and an invitation to appear on a talk show.

Not a classy talk show, mind you, but still, it was a talk show. She said yes until she found out the show was about "Moms Who Get Naked: Live! Nude! Moms!" and backed out. Not because she objected to being called a mom. Or because she knew—because I'd told her so—that I'd die if she did it.

It was the "nude" thing.

"I've never done any nude work!" she said to her agent. "I'm an artist, an actress—all right, yes, the ad. But I was wearing a pizza box! I want to be taken seriously. What about getting me on the talk show with the woman who says 'Wow!' all the time and gives her audience free cars? I could talk to her."

The "Wow!" lady wasn't interested, Mom's new agent stopped calling, and today, when we go to the supermarket, *Celeb Weekly* doesn't have her picture in it.

"I don't understand," she says. "I got so much e-mail from my fans after that interview, and they all said they'd write to the magazine and ask for more. Do you think I wasn't memorable enough?"

I look at her, dressed in a tight, bright pink T-shirt with CANDYMADISON.NET in sequins across the front, and a white skirt that barely skims the tops of her thighs. Her shoes have heels that could probably be used to pierce things.

"You're very memorable, Mom. Did you get the bread?"

"I don't eat bread." Is she pouting? It's hard to tell. She's had a lot of chemicals injected into her face.

"I know, but I do," I say, and take the *Celeb Weekly* she thrusts at me.

"Sorry," she says. "I'm just in a bad mood. They could have at least run one picture!"

"I know, but they . . ." I say, and trail off because there's Mom, in the back of the magazine under "Fashion Disasters!" The picture of her they're running was taken at the premiere of a play she did way (way) off Broadway a week ago. The play ran for exactly one night. She played a nun (now you see why the play lasted one night) and wore a dress with what she called "strategic cutouts" to a party afterward.

The caption under the picture reads, "Note to Candy Madison: Sometimes pizza boxes ARE more flattering!"

"What?" Mom says, trying to look at the magazine again. "Did I miss something? Is there a picture of me? Or, wait—is Jackson in there?"

"Um . . . Jackson," I tell her, and she looks at me, then pulls the magazine out of my hands and sees the picture.

And then she starts jumping up and down. Never mind that everyone in the grocery store is watching her even more than they usually do, most with resigned "Oh, why must she live HERE" expressions on their faces, and a few with "Oh, I hope she jumps higher because that skirt is covering less and less" grins.

"I'll go get the bread," I say, and get away. She'll be done jumping when I get back because she'll have seen the caption. At least this means we won't have to buy ten copies of the magazine.

I would rather have food than look at pictures of celebrities. (Call me crazy, but I just think it's a better choice.)

I am glad it was a picture of Mom (though I wish it was a better one) because I would so rather look at her than Jackson James, founder of jacksonjamesonline.com, the home of JJ's Girls, and current star of *JJ: Dreamworld*. He's 72, acts like he's 22, and once upon a time Mom had a child with him. Check out any online encyclopedia (or gossip site) if you don't believe me. The photo you see—and it's always the same photo—is of me and Jackson. It was taken when I was a baby, but still. It's out there.

When I get back, Mom has seen what they said about her, but still wants a copy of the magazine.

"I don't think that many people look at the captions, do you?" she says as we're heading out into the parking lot, stroking the glossy cover of *Celeb Weekly*. "I can't believe I'm in here again." Her smile is so beautiful, so glowing. So happy.

Mom almost never looks happy. Not really.

"I bet plenty of people will see the picture," I say, which isn't a lie. I'm sure plenty of people will. But I bet they'll read what's under it too. She doesn't need to hear that, though. Not now. I put the last of the groceries in her car and say, "I'll see you after work, okay?"

She nods, and when she hugs me, I tug her shirt down.

two

When you're a 17-year-old girl living in a town famous for nothing but its proximity to the interstate and enormous collection of strip malls and subdivisions, there aren't a lot of high-powered job opportunities.

There are, however, many—many—jobs in the fast food industry, and one of them is mine. I work for BurgerTown USA (a division of PhenRen Co., which makes fertilizer—tell me that doesn't make you think twice about your BurgerTown Big Bite) as a drive-thru order specialist.

In other words, people tell me what they want to eat, I type in the appropriate code/key, and then read them their automated total. The catch is, I don't actually do it at the restaurant.

When you go to a BurgerTown in New York or California or

Massachusetts or Wyoming or Georgia (really, anywhere except Hawaii and Alaska), your drive-thru order comes to a call center like mine, and I'm the one who takes your request for extra-large fries.

Well, me or one of my moronic coworkers (this doesn't include Josh).

BurgerTown has these call centers because of "cost-efficiency," which basically means they want on-site BurgerTown employees—the ones stuck in the actual restaurants—to have more time available to wipe off tables. Or mop floors. Or clean bathrooms. Management is very proud of the fact that they no longer need to hire outside cleaning crews.

Needless to say, on-site BurgerTown employees don't like us call center employees much. Mom once mentioned I worked for BurgerTown when she was cheating on her diet of the moment by eating fries, but reported that, "The girl who took my order made a face when I said you worked in the call center."

"Did your food taste funny?" I asked.

"Funny how?" Mom said. "Hey, have you seen my red, white, and blue thong?"

"Never mind," I said, but if I ever go to BurgerTown—which I won't, because I'm so sick of asking people if they want fries or pies or Big Bite combos that the thought of eating there makes me not hungry, which usually takes some serious effort—I wouldn't say I worked at the drive-thru center. Ever.

Why?

Well, you see, saying something like that is a surefire way to get the BurgerTown special—the spit meal.

We even have a secret code for it at the center. When some-one's a real ass, the kind of person who says, "Now, what kind of meat do you use in your hamburgers? Will my tomato be fresh? Oh, and I want two pieces of lettuce, not one. And make it fast, 'cause I'm in a hurry!" we put in their order and then hit**.

It's just one of those things you find out after you've worked at BurgerTown for a while (all right, a day) and everyone does it.

Well, not everyone.

Josh, my coworker and soul mate (though he doesn't know it yet) says that eating at BurgerTown is punishment enough.

"All that meat and grease and saturated fat destroys your body," he says, and I totally agree with him, really, but sometimes after I've dealt with a total jerkass who thinks ordering $4 worth of food means I owe them an ingredient reading or whatever—well, sometimes they still get the special.

Finn gives them too, which really does mean I should stop because Finn is so—well, he's your average 17-year-old Slaterville male, and they can be described in one word. Bleagh. Unlike Josh, Finn's interests don't include making plans to help others, and as far as I can tell, his favorite thing to do is be annoying, especially to me. I'm pretty good at ignoring him.

"Anyone seen Polly today?" he asks. "Josh? Hannah?"

Josh and I shake our heads and Finn grins at me. "She must be on break."

I laugh. (Okay, I'm mostly pretty good at ignoring Finn.)

Josh doesn't laugh, and I sigh, wishing I could be serious like him. But the Polly thing is funny. She's always "on break" because even though she supposedly works here, she's actually only been here a couple of times. I can understand why she doesn't come in, though. She's 22, her claim to fame is that she was once home-coming queen, and now she works (well, "works") here. Some life.

She gets away with never being here because her father, Greg, is our boss, and I think he's afraid to call her out on how she doesn't work because it would mean discussing Polly's favorite activity, which is hanging out with her 47-year-old married boyfriend, whose wife just happens to be Greg's wife's younger sister.

It's like a soap opera, only more boring because Polly is about as smart as a sponge and Greg spends his workday sitting in his closet of an office smoking pot.

Adults are so classy.

"That'll be $10.22," Josh says, and smiles at me as he checks to make sure the order went through. I guess he doesn't think I'm awful for laughing about Polly. Good.

I know I've already mentioned this, but Josh really is my soul mate. He's smart, kind, and, best of all, isn't a complete dog like every other guy in the whole world.

Josh cares about things. He writes poetry (I've seen him working on it in Government), and is always going to coffee shops for political/social discussions.

He even reads—he's always carrying around huge novels with tiny print and the kind of covers you only see on books you have to read for school. But he reads them because he cares about his mind. I love that.

He's also pretty cute.

Okay, he's gorgeous. Hard-not-to-stare-at gorgeous. He's got black hair and deep brown eyes and the most beautiful smile. Plus he's tall—but not too tall—and thin (but not scrawny), and he's just. so. out. of. my. league.

Josh doesn't date girls like me. He dates tall, skinny, dark-haired girls who care about political causes and social injustice and wear short, gauzy dresses that I could never get away with wearing. Ever. Plus they always have cool names like Arugula or Micah.

Hannah is not a cool name. Hannah is an ordinary name.

I actually wish Hannah was my only name.

But it isn't. My mother, in all her "wisdom"—and because she was facing a paternity suit—named me Hannah Jackson James. Before I moved to Slaterville, I never thought about my name. It hadn't mattered before. Not at school, and definitely not to Mom or José, who was my stepfather. I even . . . well, I even sort of liked it.

I didn't like it when we moved here. Jackson was more popular back then; his website and his castle and his collection of girlfriends weren't quite the joke they are now, but in Slaterville, which prides itself on being a sunny, welcoming community (there are actually signs when you get off the interstate)—well, let's just say some people didn't want Jackson James' former girlfriend or his kid around.

Mom didn't care—she was dealing with other stuff then—but me? I cared. Teachers raised eyebrows. Kids in my new seventh-grade classes said—well, they said a lot of things. Mostly about Jackson, which didn't bother me because, by then, I hated him.

But some of the stuff was about Mom, and that did bother me.

It went away after a while. Not until I'd had a miserable time in seventh and eighth grade, not until I'd decided to become invisible girl, but it did go away. And now, if someone does say something, I can handle it.

The thing is, though, I would love a normal mom. A mom with a job that doesn't involve sitting around in her underwear reminiscing about how one time she and Jackson went to a club and had sex on the dance floor, or how she got the pizza ad. (The director had a picture of her from *Cowboy Dad* as his computer's desktop wallpaper when he was a kid.)

But I don't have a normal mom. And when we first moved to Slaterville, all Mom had was a broken heart and me, and after a while she did what she thought she had to. What she knew. And that involved a web cam, underwear, and charging $24.95 a month to join "The Candy Club."

I used to wish we'd move back to New York, back to Queens, but now I'm glad we didn't. Jackson goes to Manhattan a lot more than he used to, seeking excitement and/or plotlines for his television show, and I don't want to be anywhere near him.

"Hannah, you've got an order," Finn says, and nudges me with his big horse feet.

"I know," I say, even though I'd missed the beep that signals them, and start my spiel. "Welcome to BurgerTown, home of the Better Burger! What can I get you today?"

When I'm done, Finn nudges my foot again.

"What are you thinking about?"

"You, of course."

"Really?" He grins at me.

"Oh yeah. I'm thinking about you and your big-ass feet stomping all over mine. It's awesome."

"Oh. Well, you, um . . . you know what they say about big feet," he says, and then blushes. It's the one thing he does that's almost endearing. Almost.

"Yes. No brain," I say, and he blushes more.

"I'm going to get a soda," he mumbles. "Want one?"

"Nah," I say, even though I do, and watch him get up. Finn is barely an inch taller than I am, and on my first day, Greg said we should sit next to each other since our hair and heights almost matched.

That should give you an idea of his "management style," and explain why Polly is able to get away with . . . well, everything.

Finn and I do have similar hair, I guess. We're both blond, but Finn's hair is dark blond, and mine is lighter, the shade Jackson's used to be. (Actually, it still is, but he's 72, so you know he dyes it.)

We also both have blue eyes, although mine are dark blue, just like Jackson's again, and Finn's are light blue. They're actually not bad-looking—Teagan even says Finn is hot, but what does she know? She doesn't have to work with him.

"You know," Finn says, leaning over my terminal, "one day you're going to ask me out. We're meant to be together. It's fate. Like peanut butter and jelly."

"Like peanut butter and jelly? For real? Finn, when's the last time you ate?"

"I am kind of hungry," he says, blushing again. "But I'm telling you, you and me—"

12

"Meant to be stuck sitting next to each other. Believe me, I know that. Now go get your soda and eat something. And never mention anything involving fate and sandwiches again."

"Deal," Finn says, and ambles off to the vending machines. We have a "break room," complete with a moldering sofa and matching chair, but nobody ever goes in there because you have to punch in your employee code to open the door—and to close it again—and however long you stay gets taken out of your pay. We're all supposed to go in there if we work eight-hour shifts, but when you're getting paid crap, you don't take breaks. Or at least, not unpaid ones.

"Order at Finn's station," Josh says, and I drift for a second, letting his voice wash over me. He even sounds good. His voice is soft, and he has this way of making everything sound meaningful. I could listen to him talk all day.

"Hannah, I'm sort of busy here," he says, and gestures at his own terminal, and I realize he means someone needs to get the order.

"Sorry," I say, and slide into Finn's chair. Slipping on his headset, I say those magic words. "Welcome to BurgerTown, home of the Better Burger! What can I get you today?"

I switch Finn's orders over to my terminal while I'm punching in an order for three chicken sandwiches, and give the total as I'm sliding back into my own seat, my headset settling into place as the customer drives off to pick up his BurgerTown Tasty Chicken Sandwiches.

"Lull," Josh says, and I nod, tossing Finn's headset back onto his seat. I would put a knot in the cord, but the last time I did that, Finn smushed his chair right up next to mine and started making static noises every time I took an order, and all my customers thought they weren't being heard.

It was actually sort of funny, but then Josh pointed out that he'd ended up having to take most of the orders. "Some of us don't mind working," he said, glancing at Finn, "but it's not fair to not do anything."

"Unless you're Polly," Finn said. "Then it's fair. Which means there's a flaw in your argument. Plus someone has to do something to keep us all from dying of boredom."

Josh just shook his head sort of sadly, which I loved. I wish I could deal with Finn like that, but I lack Josh's ability to shrug off Finn's general annoyingness.

"I love this time of day," Josh says—talking to me, he's talking to me!—and I try to think of the right thing to say.

"I love you" sounds a little intense for the conversation.

"Can we make out?" sounds like something Jackson would say, and even if I am thinking it, I never want to sound like Jackson. Ever.

"Me too," is what I come up with.

Brilliant, right?

"I can't believe I have to meet Micah after this," Josh says. "I'm tired, and I've got a ton of homework to do."

"Me too. Not meeting Micah, I mean. But the homework thing," I babble, and Josh smiles at me.

Ahhhhhhhhhhhh. It's almost enough to make me forget about Micah and how she's waiting for him.

Almost. Micah is Josh's girlfriend, and she's dark-haired and intense and plays the guitar and has political/social stickers plastered all over her car and can get away with wearing tiny floaty patchwork dresses. You know, the kind of thing you can only pull off if you have a long, lean, effortlessly ethereal look.

I don't have that look. I look like I could be a stripper, or would if I wore my hair down and didn't always make sure my shirts were big enough to hide the fact that I sprouted breasts in ninth grade. (Until then, I was like a board.)

Mom says I should be proud of my body and not hide it because when I'm her age, I'll have to actually work to keep it, meaning I won't be able to eat whatever I want and will get wrinkles like normal people do.

Mom didn't hide her body when she was my age, and she ended up with Jackson.

You can probably guess what I think of her "advice."

"Oh hey, catch," Josh says, and tosses me a small box. He grins at me. "I remember you said the vending machine was out of these the other day, and so I figured . . ."

"Animal crackers," I say, hoping I don't sound giddy, but really, this means something, right? It has to.

"What are you so happy about?" Finn asks, coming back in and flopping down into his chair. "Hey, thanks for taking my orders."

"Josh got me animal crackers," I say, and smile at Josh. "Thank you so much."

"It's nothing," Josh says. "I just saw them and thought of you."

"So Hannah reminds you of a zoo animal?" Finn asks.

Josh just shakes his head—so perfect!

I, however, am not, and kick Finn.

"What? It was just a question."

I wonder what would have happened if Finn hadn't come back when Josh gave me the cookies, or better yet, if he'd gotten crushed by one of the vending machines and I never had to see him again. I also eat all the animal crackers and try to figure out a way to save the box without looking like I'm trying to save it.

I know, it's stupid, but I just want something to remember about Josh giving me a gift.

I can't think of a way to keep the box that isn't totally obvious, but I do save a piece of it, tucking it into my bag. I glance over at Josh as I do, to see if he's watching, but he's busy at his terminal.

He doesn't look at me for the rest of our shift.

Maybe the animal crackers don't mean anything. Maybe he's just being nice. Why does he have to be so amazing? Why can't he like me? Besides the me not being his type thing, that is. And him being too smart to ever be interested in Jackson James and Candy Madison's daughter. Why couldn't Mom be a social activist? And why couldn't Jackson be . . . well, how come I have to be related to him?

If José had been my dad, life would have been so much better.

"Goodnight," Josh says as we all head out into the parking lot at exactly 10:01, when our shift ends, and I think he smiles at me.

"Bye, and thanks again," I call out, and watch as he gets in his car.

"Careful, you're drooling," Finn says. "Is your crapbucket going to start, or do I need to hang around and jump the battery again?"

"My truck is not a crap . . ." I say, and trail off. It is a crap-bucket, but it was cheap, and all I could afford. "It's running fine, and I'm not drooling."

"How come you like Josh so much anyway? All he does is sit around drinking overpriced coffee and bitching about how awful things are."

"He cares about the world."

"If he cared about the world, he'd donate the ten thousand dollars he must spend on coffee every year to charity. That would be doing something."

"And what are you doing to help people? Oh, right. Nothing."

"Hey, I don't run around claiming I'm going to change the world or—"

"Exactly."

"Can I finish?"

"I don't know. Can you?"

Finn laughs. "I was going to say, if I want to do something, I do it. I don't have to announce it to everyone."

"Except during football season. Oh, wait, I forgot. You don't play."

"Hey, I can't control the fact that people are scared of my natural talent. Besides, I figure it's easier to let everyone else do the work."

I roll my eyes at him. "Bye, Finn."

"You're sure your truck's going to start?"

"One time it didn't, ONE, and you have to bring it up all the time," I say, and unlock my door. It opens with a creaking groan, and Finn says, "Sounding good, as always," before he ambles over to his own car, which is new(ish) and also has a paint job that is all one color.

"You better start, damn you," I whisper to the truck as I slide the key into the ignition, and thankfully, it does. I head out of the parking lot, Finn behind me, and turn right, heading toward the mall.

I can't wait to see Teagan. She'll know if what happened means something.

three

"Yes," Teagan says after I've picked her up and told her all about Josh and the animal crackers.

"Yes, it means something and he likes me, or yes, I understand that he gave you food?"

"Come on, Hannah. He remembered something you said days ago and bought it for you? That's the ultimate adorable guy behavior."

"See, that's just it. Josh is adorable all the time. So was he just being his usual adorable self, or was it extra adorable in the 'I like you' way?"

"Must you overanalyze everything?" Teagan says, propping her feet against the dashboard. "If some cute guy bought me anything, I'd be . . . well, I wouldn't be getting a ride home with you, that's for sure."

"Yes, you would."

She sighs. "You're right. I'm a wuss. I'm also supposed to be figuring out a way to sell twenty pairs of jeans tomorrow night. How can I do that? I can't force people to buy stuff!"

"You can too. I've seen you in action, remember? Ten shirts in ten minutes, and those shirts were ugly."

"True," Teagan says, and fiddles with her seat belt. "Hey, remember that dress I started last month? The one I showed you the sketches for?"

I nod. Teagan makes clothes—amazing clothes, actually, like the stuff you see in magazines with a price of $5,000 listed in tiny print. She even went to college to study fashion design in Manhattan, but had to come home after a year when her mother needed to have a hip replaced.

"Well, I finished it last night," she says. "Which makes yet another outfit that'll sit in my closet. I suck."

"You don't suck. And . . . well, okay, call me crazy, but why don't you just wear the stuff you make?"

"Where would I wear it? Work?" She gestures at her jeans and shirt. "Remember, dress code?"

"What about somewhere that isn't work?"

"Like I go anywhere else. Wait . . . there is grocery shopping with my parents! Somehow, though, I just can't see myself dressing up for that. And besides, this is Slaterville, not New York, and everyone my age—"

"Oh, like you're so ancient at nineteen. You could wear the dress to . . ." I trail off. Teagan's right. Not only does Slaterville suck in terms of things to do, but when Teagan's not at work, she's at home with her parents or hiding out in her room sketching and sewing.

"Exactly," Teagan says. "I go nowhere. I am nowhere. Which is fine, because I have no talent."

"Quit it. You've got wads of talent. Wait, that sounds strange. Lots of talent. You have lots of talent. People don't go to New York to study fashion unless they have it."

"Okay, enough about me," Teagan says, dropping her feet off the dashboard. "I'll bring you some gas money tomorrow. I know I owe you."

I wave a hand at her. "I've got enough in the crapbucket for a few more trips. Besides, it's not like you live a thousand miles away from me."

"And yet I've never been to your house."

"You know my rule. Nobody comes in the house, not even you. The last thing I need is people seeing Mom in her . . . natural state."

"It's that bad?"

"Do you want to see your mother walking around in her underwear all the time?"

"Point," Teagan says. "Hey, what did Finn say about the whole animal cracker thing?"

"Oh, he was his usual self. Plus he's still reminding me about the one time he had to jump the truck's battery. Every night, it's 'Do you think your truck will start?'"

"Crap, my parents are waiting up for me," Teagan says, looking out the window. "See them lurking in the kitchen?"

"You mean sitting at the table, talking to each other and

not even looking out here? Yeah, I see that. Great lurking."

"Funny," she says. "Now tell me what you're going to say to Josh at work tomorrow."

"Thanks for the animal crackers?"

"Didn't you already say that?"

"Yeah, twice. I'm pathetic."

"You're not pathetic," Teagan says. "Why don't you ask him what he's doing over the weekend?"

I'm silent for a second as I pull to a stop by her house, and then I look at her.

We both burst into giggles.

"Oh yeah," I say. "And then I'll give him my phone number! And tell him to call me! Please."

"Okay, okay," Teagan says. "What about . . . oh! I know! What does he like to eat?"

"Four-buck mocha lattes."

"Get him one of those. Like, buy yourself one and get a second and say you were getting one and thought of him, like he did with you."

"Ooooh, I like that," I say. "But I hate coffee. You know that."

"Stop being dense on purpose. Get a hot chocolate or something."

"But what if he—?"

"What? Asks you out? Says he likes you? Oh no!"

"All right, fine. I'll buy him coffee."

"Wow, look at you being talked into something you want to do. It's a miracle!"

"Ha ha." I elbow her.

She grins at me, gets out of the truck, and then turns back toward me. "I mean it! Buy him coffee!"

I wave at her as I drive off, and try to picture buying coffee for Josh. I can see myself doing it, sort of.

But actually giving him the coffee? That I can't see. What if he said he didn't want it? Then I'd look like an idiot.

When I get home, Mom's sitting at the kitchen table, wearing a silver bikini and eating a piece of toast.

"Since when are you eating bread again?" I ask. Mom's ever-changing diets are a real pain because I like food, plus I hate watching her live on things like rice cakes and lettuce. It just seems so stupid. I mean, what's so bad about real food?

"I'm starving," she says. "I just finished doing a chat with this group of programmers. They're all huge fans of *Cowboy Dad*, and one of them is getting married, so they all chipped in for an hour of me telling stories about the show. Oh, and get this—they were going to a strip club after, and supposedly one of the dancers looks like me. Can you believe it? I'm a stripper specialty now!"

I start to make myself a piece of toast. It's easier than saying anything.

She sighs. "I'm telling you, it's very flattering. I haven't had strippers try for my look since I was with Jackson."

Now it's my turn to sigh. As much as I'm embarrassed by Mom sometimes (okay, most of the time), I love her, and I know this sudden spurt of sort-of-fame has made her feel good for the first time in years.

"It's great, Mom."

"Thank you," she says with a wry smile. "How was work?"

"The usual. Hey, did you get your check for last month yet?"
She nods.

"And?" I look at her. Since Mom works online, everyone pays through a payment site that Mom doesn't run—and that takes a cut of everything she gets.

"And I did okay. And yes, before you ask, I can pay all the bills."

"You're supposed to be saving for retirement too. Remember?"

"You act like I'm sixty," she says. "I've got plenty of time."

"Well, if you need me to help out, I can go to the bank before I go to work tomorrow."

"Oh no," she says, getting up and adjusting her top. "I'm not taking your money. I've never taken a handout from Jackson, and I'm certainly not taking one from you. And now I gotta get back to work. Do I look okay?"

"Hey, strippers are copying you now, right?" I say, and she squeezes my shoulder before sashaying out of the room and into the den, closing the door behind her.

I eat another piece of toast and then go upstairs to do my homework. When I go to bed at one, Mom is still up, and I fall asleep listening to the sound of her laughter, sunny and sweet and fake.

She's faked being happy for so long I've almost forgotten what she sounds like when she's happy for real.

Almost.

four

When me and Mom came to Slaterville, she was as down as I've ever seen her. Destroyed, really. We drove into town on a whim; her, me, and José's ashes tucked into an engraved metal box in the backseat, and stayed.

I didn't think we would at first; Mom was in a bad place then, a place that kept us moving, always moving, but we did. We stayed and Mom bought us a little house with the money from José's insurance policy, but in our first year here, when she'd tried (and failed) to find local acting work, she ran up huge credit card bills. After that, she had to remortgage the house.

And after she paid off all the bills, there was enough left for her to have the website built.

The rest is history, more than two-thirds of it available for (paid) download on her site.

Do I miss how things were when we lived with José? How things were before he died, when it was the three of us and life was . . . well, normal? Definitely. But I know Mom does too, and that makes it easier.

Not better, though. As much as I hate seeing old footage of her—even *Cowboy Dad*, which wasn't that bad (for a crap sitcom, anyway)—at least then she wasn't . . .

Well, you try having a mother whose job is hanging around in her underwear in front of a web cam.

She says she likes it, and I think she does, mostly. Mom is proud of her body, and loves working at home. Going to the grocery store is about the most social thing she does.

Other than the talking to people in her underwear thing, that is.

I know things won't magically change when I go to college— one more year at Slaterville High left, just one more—but at least then I'll have some distance between me and Mom, just like now I have some distance between me and Jackson. And while I love Mom, I'm tired of how her choices shape my so-called life.

For instance, when I leave for school the next morning, I see our next-door neighbor, Mrs. Howard. As soon as she sees me, she twitches her kitchen curtains shut.

Like I'm a blight on society in my baggy jeans and shirt whose cuffs extend down over my hands. Like I'm going to rip off all my clothes and run around the yard naked.

Jackson wouldn't even do something like that. He'd get one of his girlfriends to do it—and they would, too—but he'd never do it. Mom wouldn't do it either, but she also doesn't notice stuff like Mrs. Howard—or if she does, she ignores it when I'm around. I can't ignore it, though.

I see it, and I hate it.

I give Mrs. Howard the finger before I get in the crapbucket, and I know she sees me too, because the curtains twitch again.

Good.

School is school. Middle school—I got to Slaterville about halfway through seventh grade—was hell, but I've spent so long trying to be invisible that now I am. I mean, I know people . . . well, okay. One person.

Michelle. She's been in at least two of my classes every year since I moved here, and sometimes we talk, but that's it. Once in a while I wonder what it would be like to have a friend I could really talk to, or at least eat lunch with, but since Teagan and I started hanging out last year, I don't think about it so much.

I met Teagan last spring. I'd seen her around before she went to college, of course, but she was a senior who wore amazing clothes and talked about going to New York all the time. And I was—and did—none of those things.

But last spring, I was sitting outside one night while Mom was working, trying to pretend I didn't care that the Howards were looking at me out their windows every five seconds like I was about to start writhing around on the grass or something, and Teagan walked by.

"Hey," she said, and I was so surprised that she was back home—and, all right, that she'd spoken to me—that I said "Hey" back. We ended up talking for a couple of hours, and I learned she'd just come back from New York to help out after her mother's hip surgery, and that she wasn't thrilled to be back in Slaterville.

"I just hate this place so much," she said. "It's so . . . I don't know. Soul-sucking. And why are your neighbors staring at us like that?"

I tensed. "Because they're the Howards. And . . . well, you know who my mom is, right?"

"Oh," she said. And then—and this is what made me really like her—she said, "Wait, for real, that's why? Haven't you guys been here for, like, years? Man, the Howards must have no lives at all. Not that your mom isn't interesting or whatever. It's just— well, come on. Isn't there something else they could do? At the very least, Mrs. Howard could buy some new clothes. Someone should tell her big shoulder pads only look good if you're a foot-ball player."

How could I not like her after that? And when her mom came home from the hospital, and needed physical therapy and couldn't do as much as she used to, Teagan stayed. She started working full-time at the mall a few months ago, and I'm guessing she's saving up to get out of town, go back to New York and school. She hasn't said for sure, but then that's Teagan. She hardly ever talks about New York. I don't blame her. Being here after being there, being here after following your dream? It must be hard. I'm going to miss her when she leaves.

But for now, at least, I have a friend, and so in school I mostly just wonder what it would be like to do high school things. To go out on the weekends, and not just to work or the grocery store with my mother. To kiss a guy.

To have a normal life. A real one.

five

I have one class with Josh, and it's the best part of my day.

I wish I had all my classes with him, so I could sit near him and look at the back of his neck and then imagine him turning around and getting up and coming over to me and—

Anyway, I just have the one class. Government.

Today, Josh is writing. If I sit leaning forward and all the way to the right, so I'm smushing myself into the side of my desk, I can just make out a bit of his notebook page.

It's not the most comfortable pose, but I can see actual words, and he seems to be writing about love because I see the words "heart" and "mind."

I also see the word "Fyodor," which confuses me until I

remember that lately Josh has been reading *The Brothers Karamazov*. I actually bought a copy after I first saw him with it, thinking that I'd read it and we could talk about it.

I didn't get very far. The print was tiny and what I read seemed to be sort of a story and sort of a lot of thoughts about complicated things like human nature. I honestly didn't see it as any kind of love story, but then Josh reads big thick books on a regular basis and I don't.

And what Josh writes . . . well, I've never seen it, other than the glimpses I've gotten in class, but I can tell it's poetry because he never writes more than a page, and a couple of times I've made out rhyming words.

Could he be more perfect? Smart, sweet, hot—and writes poetry? I have to buy him coffee today. It won't be that hard.

I write "BUY COFFEE!" in my notebook, to make it more real, and a crumpled-up ball of paper lands on my desk. I don't have to guess who it's from. I sit in the back of the class, in the very last chair on the left-hand side of the room—it's my favorite place to sit in all my classes.

But in this one, Finn sits across from me.

I wish he was up front, where a couple of jock and jock-followers sit, but no, he's here, and has been since he got moved for talking about a week after I started at BurgerTown.

"What are you doing?" his note says. Finn used to try to talk to me outside of work sometimes, used to come up to me here, in school, but he'd turn all red and I'd get pissed that he was embarrassed to be talking to me and walk off so I wouldn't smack him, and after a while he gave up.

Then the notes started. At first they drove me crazy because he'd say stuff like, "Hey, are you actually taking notes?" like he knew me or something. Like he cared, or whatever.

I ignored him, but they kept coming, and the fifth note he ever tossed me was a list of all the BurgerTown order codes. Greg had said he'd get me one on my first day (still haven't actually seen an official one), and if it hadn't been for Finn writing down that "cc" meant "cash" and "cd" meant "credit card," I'd still be screwing up orders.

So the day after he gave me the codes, when he tossed a piece of paper that said, "Ten bucks Polly doesn't show for work today," I wrote back, "Twenty that she doesn't actually exist. PS Thx for the codes."

He actually made me pay him the twenty when Polly showed up at work for ten minutes the next week, but gave it back when our shift was over, saying that since she hadn't actually spoken, her existence was still in doubt, or, in his words, "Did you see how she didn't talk? I'm thinking she's probably a ghost. Or an elaborate computer animation. Hey, do you want this thing of cookies I bought? I thought they were chocolate chip, but they're chocolate pecan chip and I hate nuts."

"Ghosts and computer animations can't possibly wear as much perfume as she did," I said, and he laughed and I gladly took back my twenty—and the cookies. Money had been really tight then, and I'd been eating bread and mustard sandwiches at work. And at school. And at home. They tasted as bad as they sound, but Mom had been strapped because something had gone wrong with her online payment system and it had taken a few days to get fixed, and I'd still been waiting for my first Burger-Town paycheck.

Now I write back, "I'm sitting here. What does it look like I'm doing?"

"Having a seizure. I didn't know the human neck could move like that."

"Hilarious," I write back, and then the bell rings.

Coffee, I remind myself as I head into the hall, moving fast so I can catch a last, quick glimpse of Josh before he vanishes down the hall. (Well, actually into Micah's arms, but close enough.)

One mocha latte. That's all. I can do that. I will do it.

I will.

Except I don't.

I mean to, I really do, but when school gets out and I drive to work, I can't stop at the coffee place I know Josh goes to.

Or any of the other three I pass on my way to the call center.

I mean, I could stop—my truck brakes work. Mostly. But the thought of carrying the coffee in and saying, "Josh, I got this for you"—what if he already has coffee? What if he doesn't drink mocha lattes anymore? What if I buy one, offer it to him, and he says, "No thanks, I don't want it."

Then I'd know he doesn't like me.

And okay, while I'm pretty sure he doesn't like me, at least right now I can pretend that he might—and I'd like to hold on to that.

However, Josh doesn't have coffee when I get to work, and even says, "Man, I wish I'd stopped and gotten a mocha latte before I came here. I hate that the vending machines don't have anything that isn't filled with sugar or chemicals."

"Me too," I say, now wishing for a time machine so I could go back and buy the coffee after all, and then realize my can of sugar-filled cola is sitting right on top of my terminal. I lean over a little, like I'm just sort of casually slouching, and block the soda from his sight. Or at least I hope I do.

"They do have water," Finn says. "Nothing objectionable in that, right?"

"It's still money lining an overly wealthy corporation's pockets."

"True," Finn says. "Not like those struggling artists over at Coffee, Inc., with their stores every three feet and all."

"They give back to the community," Josh says, shaking his head at Finn, who snorts but says, "Okay, man, whatever."

I take advantage of the moment to move my soda to the floor, and then say, "I like the muffins at Coffee, Inc.," because I want Josh to keep talking and because I know the muffins definitely help people in need. The case has a little sign next to them that says 10 percent of the cost goes to a children's charity. Teagan says she figures that's why they charge $3.75 for them.

"They're okay," Josh says. "Not nearly as good as animal crackers, though."

That means something, right? I think it must.

And then he smiles.

My insides go all melty and I vow I'll buy him coffee tomorrow for sure. And ask him what he's doing on Saturday, and—

And then he picks up his book and starts reading.

Forget the coffee. I read way too much into everything. Josh was just talking, which plenty of people do, and I have to remember that. Sigh.

Why is this all so hard? Why does he have to be so perfect and sweet? Why?

Why can't he like me?

"Still reading about the Russian guys, huh?" Finn says.

"Second time through," Josh says, giving Finn a patient look. "It says so much you have to read it more than once to really understand it."

"Oh, right, like—hold on," Finn says, and takes an order. I get one too, and when I'm done, I practically rip off my headset because Josh is talking again and I know he's saying something intense. I can tell because his forehead is all squinched up. He only does that when he's talking about something meaningful.

I bet he looks like that when he reads his poetry. I bet Micah gets to hear his poetry. I wish I was her.

"It's about a lot of things," Josh is saying. "It's—the book addresses universal themes. That's what makes it great literature."

"Totally," I say, because even if I didn't really get the book— or read most of it—I know he must be right.

Josh smiles at me again. "You've read it?"

I nod, and hope he doesn't ask me about it. Or at least about anything that happens after the first fifty pages.

"Oh, I get what you're saying now," Finn says. "Like how when Fyodor's wife dies, there's that whole line about how some people see him doing one thing and some see him doing another, but only one thing is true?"

"Exactly," Josh says, and I stare at him because I remember that part and that's not what I thought happened at all. After Fyodor's wife dies, some people see him doing one thing—being sad—and some see him doing another—being happy—and both could be true because he was glad to be free from her and sorry that she'd died.

I got that part because it sounded exactly like something Jackson would do.

"I didn't know you'd read the book," Josh says, sounding surprised.

"I can read," Finn says. "Sometimes I can even spell complicated words like f-a-k-e-r."

See, here's where I'd yell. But Josh doesn't. He just smiles—a little snarkily, but who can blame him?—and says, "So which emotion do you think was the true one?"

"Both," Finn says after a moment. "There's that whole thing about people being more naive and simple-hearted than we think, right?"

Josh shrugs and turns back to his terminal, his expression pinched-looking, and I can tell he knows Finn is right.

"Here," Finn says, picking my soda up off the floor and handing it to me.

"That's not mine," I say.

"Yeah, it is. I saw you come in with it and put it—"

"No, it's not mine," I say, glancing at Josh. Please don't let him be watching this.

"Oh," Finn says, and puts the soda back down. I look at

him—it's okay, Josh isn't even looking at me—and Finn frowns and turns back to his terminal.

I sort of expected more of a fight from Finn because we both know it is my soda, but that's okay. Good, even. And when he gets a customer, I slide my chair toward Josh's.

"Hey," I say, and he looks at me.

"Hey." He still looks a little upset.

"I just . . . I think it's really cool that you read, you know? In public, I mean. Every other guy around here, all they talk about is sports and their cars and stuff like that. You talk about real things."

"Thanks," Josh mumbles, and then he smiles at me. A beautiful smile that makes my knees go weak even though I'm sitting down. "I know sometimes I kind of go on, but there's so much more to life than Slaterville."

"Which is a very good thing."

"Absolutely," he says. "I like to think of life as a chance to explore everything, you know? Do you—?"

"Hannah, you've got an order."

Why does Finn have to work here? Why?

"I know," I say through gritted teeth, even though I didn't, and slide back over to my terminal.

The person ordering takes forever to decide what kind of diet soda she wants with her salad and then changes her order to a triple cheeseburger and onion rings at the last minute. When I've finally finished and look up from my terminal, Josh has left the room.

Damn!

"He'll be back," Finn says. "He had to go get some coffee. And probably find someone to explain the book he's supposedly reading to him so he can 'go on' about exploring life or whatever."

"So now you're listening to my conversations?"

"It's not like I've got anyone else to listen to," Finn says, but his face is turning red. "And look, I get that you like him or whatever, but you know he just acts like he cares about stuff, right? If he actually did care, wouldn't he do more than sit around drinking coffee?"

"He does things," I say. "He goes to meetings."

"Meetings? Oh, you mean how he goes and drinks coffee and talks about how much he cares and the big mystery of life? You're right. He's practically a saint."

"And you're doing so much to help with—what is it again? Oh, right. Nothing."

"Hey," he says, leaning toward me. "You can care without telling everyone. I mean, don't you think that really caring about someone—something—is about actually doing stuff and not just talking about it?"

"Sure. But you—"

"Hannah," he says, "do you really think I can't care about stuff? About people?"

"I . . ." I say, suddenly very aware of how close he is and how we are all alone and how, up close, his eyes are actually more blue-gray than blue. And how my body doesn't seem to notice that I am not looking at Josh, my soul mate, but Finn, who drives me crazy.

"Hannah," he says again, and I have never noticed Finn's

mouth (well, maybe a little), but it's a nice mouth, especially when it's curved like it is now, like he might be thinking about my mouth, like he might be—

"Hey, we've got orders backed up," Josh says, and I see him standing in the doorway, looking kind of pissed.

six

"Didn't you see the lights flashing?" he asks, and I shake my head as Finn says, "Hey, at least some of us were here."

"Fine, whatever, I'll take care of it," Josh says, and sits down.

Is he mad? I think he might be. But why is he mad? Because we've got backed up orders, or because he saw Finn and me . . . looking at each other?

Either way, I start taking orders immediately, and try not to stare at Josh too much.

I must not do a very good job, though, because when things have slowed down, he looks at me, smiles, and says, "Hey, Hannah, I got you something."

"You did?" I hear my voice squeak and know I sound stupid, but I don't care. He's giving me something else, he must like me!

He passes me a white paper bag, and I open it. Inside is a small box of chocolate-covered peppermints.

Ick. I hate mint.

Still, I smile and say, "Thank you," because duh, he's given me something else. And I can always give the candy to Mom. She loves these things. She won't eat them, but she might smell them or something. I don't even want to do that.

"It's for being so nice before," he whispers, sliding over next to me, and I eat one of the mints just so he'll stay right where he is for a little while longer.

Ugh. Even chocolate can't disguise the fact that this so-called candy tastes like toothpaste. How Mom can list them as one of her favorites on the "About Me" section of her site is beyond me.

"Orders," Finn says, sounding cranky, and although normally I'd be pissed at him for interrupting Josh and me—or, at least, Josh sitting next to me while I try to finish the mint without actually tasting it—I have to say I'm not entirely sorry to be alone at my terminal.

Also, I'm going to have to talk to Teagan about what this all means.

And I'm especially going to have to talk to her because when work ends, Josh, instead of racing out into the parking lot like he usually does, walks out with me (with me!), Finn trailing behind us.

"It figures tonight was busy," he says. "I was hoping we could talk more. But in the meantime . . ." He reaches into his messenger bag, which is another thing I adore about him. Everyone carries a backpack, but not Josh. He has a cool, beat-up messenger bag, covered with stickers protesting all kinds of things.

"I thought you might like this," he says, and hands me a CD. The case has a typed list of songs.

Okay, even I know *this* means something. I look down at the song titles, trying to figure out if they're love songs.

They aren't. It's all old stuff, like from when I was little. There is one sort of new song, though, "Discontent in Winter 4." It's one of those obscure songs that anyone who likes music is supposed to love. I know that because Mom sometimes chats with the group's drummer and she put a download link to the song on her website so they'd put a link to her on theirs.

"I know most of them are classics," Josh says, "but I like those. A great song is a forever song, you know?"

"Totally." I have got to start thinking of things to say that aren't one word. Or, at least, aren't one word that makes me sound like an idiot. "I mean, thank you. You got me cookies and the mints and . . . you didn't have to do this."

"I know," he says. "I wanted to." And then he touches my face. Right there in the parking lot, with the lights making his hair shine, and he's so close and he's touching my face, and his eyes are huge and gorgeous, and he's so gorgeous I just want to tackle him.

Take him down, right there in the parking lot, kiss the crap out of him, and then get his shirt off and slide up against him and—

Well, you get the idea. Thanks so much for the outsized libido, Jackson. I'm sometimes—all right, usually—afraid that if I ever actually do anything with a guy, I'll just . . . let's just say I worry that before you know it, I'd be walking around with five guys on my arm, calling them "my boys" and acting like an idiot.

"Hey, Josh, Micah's here," Finn says, and Josh looks over at a car idling at the edge of the parking lot, then slowly drops his hand away from my face.

"Gotta go," he says, heading off across the parking lot. Halfway to the car that's waiting for him, he turns back and waves at me.

At least I think it's at me. Finn is nearby-ish, but why would Josh wave at him? Also, he didn't give Finn a CD. Or candy.

"Okay, seriously, what is it about him?" Finn says. "How come he can flirt with you while his girlfriend is sitting in her car, waiting for him, and that's okay, but the one time a girl from another call room comes in and asks for the coupon code, you call me Pig Boy for two days?"

"That's because all you did was look down her shirt the whole time she was there."

"I didn't do that! At least, not the whole time."

"Do you really think he was flirting with me?"

"Let's see. He gave you candy you hate—I saw your face— and a CD of songs . . ." He looks at the CD. "All of these are, like, twenty years old, at least. Figures. Oh, and he groped your face. Sounds like true love to me."

"He didn't grope my face. We were talking. And he also bought me animal crackers. I like them."

"You also bitched about them not being in the vending machine for a week. Everyone in the building knows you like animal crackers."

"I don't see you bringing me any."

"Do you want me to?" Finn says, and his voice somehow

changes as he says it, the question almost sounding like he means it. For some reason, I think about earlier, and how close we were and how looking at him made me feel all wobbly even though I was sitting down.

Now, I know that a momentary flash of . . . whatever for Finn doesn't really mean anything. Or wouldn't, if I was normal. But I'm Jackson James' daughter, and sometimes I really do think that I could turn into the female version of him.

"Like you'd spare a buck fifty you could spend on yourself on anyone else, much less me," I say, and head off to my truck.

Finn waits till I've started the crapbucket before he gets into his own car, and as I watch him get in, I—all right, I admit it, I check out the way his shirt stretches along his shoulders and . . . other things. It makes me feel bad, though. Not just because it's Finn, of all people, but because I like Josh.

But I do it anyway.

It's stuff like this that scares me. That makes me think that maybe, deep down, I'm like Jackson, and I'm only ever going to be able to think about myself and sex forever and ever and ever.

I need to talk to Teagan.

seven

"So I really like Josh. I mean, really like him. And tonight was so perfect. But then there was this . . . thing with Finn. It was just for a second, but you have to promise that if I start talking about sharing my love or anything like that, you'll smack me, okay?" I tighten my hands on the steering wheel and blow out a breath, glad to finally get it all out.

Teagan laughs. "The day you start to talk about sharing your love is the day the world ends," she says. "You can't even talk to Josh without freaking out. I mean, look at you. You got two more things from Josh today, which clearly means he likes you, and what are you doing? Freaking out."

"He touched my face, too."

"Wait, what? When was this?"

"Right after work," I say, and when I finish telling her all about it, she says, "Wow. I think he was going to kiss you."

"Really?"

"Yeah. And right in front of his girlfriend. That's a little . . . well, you say he's intense, right?"

"He is. I saw him writing poetry in Government today. And he's always talking about how people need to pay attention to the world around them and—"

"Okay, he's intense. So he probably was so into you he forgot everything."

"Probably?"

"Definitely," Teagan says, but looks out the window before turning back to me. "So tell me more about this thing with Finn."

"It wasn't a thing."

"You said it was."

"It really wasn't—all right, it was," I say. "Quit staring at me! I'm trying to drive. It's way more difficult at night. Don't you know that?"

"I know you're full of it," she says. "Spill."

So I do.

"So you looked at him, and thought about you and him doing—"

"Kissing," I yelp. "Just kissing." (Okay, it was a little more. But not that much. Not really.)

"That's it?" Teagan sounds disappointed.

"That's it? It's Finn, Teagan. Finn."

"And?"

"And he . . . he plays football. I know you remember what Slaterville football players are like."

"I thought you said he sits on the bench."

"He's still on the team, though, and he hangs out with guys like Brent, the jerk who thinks running around a field slapping other guys' asses means he's better than everyone. And Finn's just . . . I don't know. He's Finn."

"You know, you sure do talk about Finn an awful lot. I mean, who are we talking about now?"

"You brought him up!"

"Okay, but considering it's pretty obvious that Josh likes you, you've spent just as much, if not more, time worrying about wanting to kiss Finn."

"Because I'm afraid it means I'm going to turn into Jackson!"

"Uh huh."

"Teagan!"

She laughs. "Look, you have to get over yourself. Tomorrow you're going to actually buy the coffee you were supposed to today, and you'll ask Josh out. And he'll say yes, and you'll go, and you'll kiss him and the world won't end. Then you can thank me and—ugh. My parents are waiting up for me again."

"I guess your mom is really doing better."

"Yeah," Teagan says, looking out the window toward her house.

"So have you asked them how much longer they want you to stay? I mean, I know you must miss New York and stuff. School."

She's silent as I stop at the end of her driveway.

"Teagan, you should tell them you think they'll be okay on their own. Then you can go, you know?"

"I will."

"When?"

"Soon."

"Tonight?"

"Soon," she says, and gets out of the truck. "See you tomorrow. And do the coffee thing already!"

I drive home, wondering if Teagan is right. Maybe the whole Finn thing was just a random . . . whatever.

Come to think of it, I am pretty hungry, and I didn't eat dinner at work because I didn't bring anything and then Josh gave me the candy and I didn't feel like I could go buy something because he'd given me food.

Then I walk inside, and spot Mom on the phone. She's wearing a pink ruffled thing, the top cut so low you can see most of her black and pink bra peeking out.

Maybe I'm right to worry. I mean, I do have a mother who basically wears underwear while talking to people she never sees for a living.

"Here," she says, turning to me and holding out the phone. "It's Jackson."

"Jackson?"

Mom nods.

I take the phone, suddenly feeling shaky. I haven't spoken to Jackson since I was twelve.

Why is he calling now?

eight

He isn't.

Fran, his longtime secretary and the woman who organizes his life for him, is.

"Hi, angel," she says. "How've you been?"

I haven't spoken to Fran since I was twelve too. When Jackson doesn't talk to someone, no one around him talks to that person either.

"Fine," I say, my voice tight. "What do you want?"

"I know it's been a long time," she says. "Too long. I've missed you. And Jackson has—hold on. You there, yes, you with the tray—Jackson didn't order a pickle with that sandwich. He never eats pickles. Go back to the kitchen and get another one. Don't just stand there. Go!"

Fran does a lot of yelling. Jackson does none. He doesn't like confrontation of any kind, so Fran handles it for him.

"Sorry about that," she says, and I hear the familiar sound of a video camera in the background and know she's being taped right now. I clench my hand tighter around the phone. "We've had to hire some new staff and they have to be trained, and anyway, what are you doing on Friday?"

"Going to school."

"Oh, of course you are. I forgot you're still in school. Seventeen now, right? A junior? Working at BurgerTown?"

"Right," I say, and try not to picture someone telling Fran all of that, try not to picture myself as part of a search run to update Jackson's "personal database." Try not to picture Fran reading all that information off one of the index cards Jackson makes her keep on everyone he's ever met before the cameras came in and she picked up the phone.

"So," Fran says. "You do know that Jackson—"

"No," I say, cutting her off. "I don't know. I don't know what Jackson's doing. Don't visit his site, don't watch his show. Why? Is he dead or something?"

I hear a soft sound, like someone clearing their throat, and know Jackson is listening in, off camera in another room. Figures. He used to always listen to every phone call because he—well, because he's Jackson. That's what he does. Just like he always clears his throat when he's nervous or upset. Right before he ignores you and/or walks away.

"He's fine," Fran says soothingly, even though we both know I didn't sound very concerned about the possibility of Jackson being dead. "I was just thinking you might like to take Friday off from school and fly up to New York, spend some time in the city with Jackson."

Jackson wants to see me. I hope for a second—I do, even though I hate that I do—and then reality kicks in.

"Ratings must be down, right?" I say to Fran. "So . . . let me guess, it's time for a reminder that Jackson James is a devoted family man. Tell the producers it's sweet of them to think of me, but I'll pass."

There's silence for a moment, and then a clicking sound, like a recording device being turned off. I grit my teeth and wait, sad and pissed off, and sure enough, a moment later, I hear Jackson's voice.

"I was hoping to tell you about the trip before Fran did, but I guess she beat me to it. We're both just so excited about seeing you again."

His voice isn't as loud as Fran's was, which means the phone call isn't being taped for the show anymore. Guess what I said must have annoyed the producers.

Good.

"No, Fran, I'll look over those photos in a minute," he says. "Right now I want to talk to my daughter."

Ha! Like Jackson would ever turn down looking at pictures of scantily clad women for anyone, even me. Especially me. How dumb are the people who watch his show? And how dumb does he think I am? Nobody's listening to the phone call anymore, but the cameras are still rolling. Pretending he wants to talk to me doesn't mean I believe he does.

Not now, anyway.

"Sorry about the interruption," Jackson says. "I'll take care of the travel arrangements, all right? And Hannah—I can't wait to see the city with you again."

I don't say anything, knowing he'll keep going. And sure enough, he does.

"I love you too," Jackson says, as smoothly as if I'd actually said it to him first, or at all. "I'd tell you how to find me when the limo brings you in from the airport and drops you at the hotel, but then I'm easy to spot—just look for all the beautiful women and I'll be there!"

Then he hangs up. Just like that, like five years of silence means nothing—and it does, it means nothing to him, and I hate that—but I force myself to make a wry face at Mom and hand the phone back to her. "Show crap."

"I figured as much when Fran asked me what I thought about the latest episode," Mom says. "Well, that and the fact that she called." She clears her throat. "It's been a while."

"Five years."

"It's a long time," Mom says, looking at me, and I grab a pen off the counter and doodle on a piece of paper, not looking at her. A little more than five years ago I was happy.

I also actually liked Jackson. I was so stupid.

"I know your last trip to see him wasn't great, but maybe—?"

"Wasn't great? Really? I hadn't noticed, even though Jackson made me look like an idiot."

"Jackson's just . . ."

"A jerk?"

"Difficult," Mom says, but she's smiling now. "Do you want to see him?"

"Nope," I say, and she nods once, the smile slipping from her face.

"Why?" I say. "Do you think I should?"

Mom adjusts the straps of her pink ruffled thing. "I think you should think about it. He's not going to be around forever, and despite . . . despite how he can be, he's a very loving and sensitive man."

"Uh huh. Would you go see him?"

"He'd never ask me."

"But if he did?"

"He'd never ask," Mom says again, her voice very quiet. "When Jackson's done with someone, he's done. And he and I—well, we didn't end very well, did we?"

She rolls her shoulders back, tosses her hair, and smiles again. "I'm going to surprise my overseas fans with a morning greeting—it's got to be morning somewhere, right?—and then I'm going to bed. See you in the real morning, okay?"

"Okay," I say, rattled by the weird heaviness of her last words, by the stuff I know she's thinking about now, and after she's left, I dump my junk on the counter, toss the mints into the pantry, and make myself a sandwich.

Mom was nineteen when she met Jackson. She moved in with him two days later, and was out of his castle—and life—by the time she was twenty-one.

I was born seven months after she moved out, and then all

the paternity stuff happened. It would be nice to not know much about it—I was a baby, after all, so it's not like I would remember, and Mom and José never talked about it (and of course Jackson never talks about anything remotely emotional)—but it was something kids in Slaterville's Grover Cleveland Middle School used to love to ask me about.

Stupid Slaterville.

I know that I'm a junior, and shouldn't still be upset about things I heard when I was younger. But you try being just-turned-thirteen and finding out that Jackson once insisted I couldn't be his kid because Mom hadn't been "arousing him" and that he was also "quite sure" she'd been having sex with anyone who asked her.

It wasn't true, of course, but hearing it still hurt, and I spent the first few weeks of school in Slaterville coming home dry-eyed (I'd sworn I wouldn't cry in front of anyone again, ever, and I'd meant it) and furious. On day twenty-one, the end of week three, I came home dry-eyed with split knuckles.

The split knuckles came from giving the bearer of all the news—Brent Wilkins, resident asshat even then—a bloody nose, and when Mom asked me what I'd done, I screamed that she might have told me that Jackson once tried to say I wasn't his back before I was even born, and that life would have been easier if she'd just told me that he'd never loved me at all.

"I wish we were still in Queens!" I said. "I wish we were still with José."

Mom closed her eyes, and kept them closed for a long time.

When she opened them again they were red and wet, filled with unshed tears. "I wish we were too," she said. "But we aren't.

And as for Jackson, yes, he did . . . he did say things. But that doesn't mean he doesn't care about you. I know your last visit didn't go well, but I'm sure he wants to see you—"

"No," I told her. "He doesn't. He won't even call. You'll see."

And Jackson didn't call, just like I'd said.

But now he had.

nine

The thing is, I used to like Jackson. I used to love him, even. Back before José died, I even called him Dad.

I didn't see Jackson often, but when I did, it was like a holiday. He lives in a castle in upstate New York, a couple of hours outside Manhattan. It's an honest-to-God castle, too, something he bought from some poor Earl or Duke and had shipped over from England and reassembled. He could have built a castle, but he wanted the real thing. The neighbors didn't like it—too big, too tacky, too over-the-top—or Jackson himself for that matter, but Jackson never cared about things like that.

He had an empire to run. A giving, caring empire where the girls who posed for his website were well compensated, and even encouraged to finish school or start their own businesses. He gave generously to charities. He went on television and argued passion-ately for universal health care, for an end to human rights violations.

He was beloved, in the way Americans embrace celebrities, and held up as a man of taste, style, and kindness.

Or at least that's how he seemed to be. And Mom swears he really was like that, at least for a few years. But then Jackson started to believe he was as great as everyone said he was, and you can guess what happened.

His first—and only—wife, the one who was his age and who'd supported him while he got the site up and running, who'd pretended not to see his roving eyes and hands because she loved him? Gone. Before the castle was even finished, before he—and she—could move in, he filed for divorce.

She died of cancer before the case ever made it to court. She'd kept how sick she was a secret to "spare him pain." He wept at her funeral and said he'd love her forever.

Four months later, he was living in the castle with the first of the five "special girls"—girls who never made it onto the site but, as he put it, "found a place in my heart." They were all dark-haired, dark-eyed, and tiny, never more than a size four. (Except for the chest, of course. That was a different story.)

His "special girls" went on TV with him when he made appearances, and after three years, four of the first ones who'd "found a place" in his so-called heart were gone, replaced by four new girls. Mom was one of those girls.

Jackson was in his fifties then, which is ancient and also dis-gusting since Mom was only nineteen, but she swears he looked and acted younger. There's a whole section in her autobiography where she talks about how handsome and active he was. I once tried to read it, but it made me feel like the insides of my eyes were bleeding.

Anyway, Mom moved in with Jackson right after they met, which was during his biggest party of the year, which, naturally, was for his birthday. She never appeared on the site, like all his other "special girls," but she did show up in Jackson's video diaries, which he put up on the site and which featured him roaming around the castle with his "special girls."

In spite of the fact that she was never actually featured on the website, Mom became a favorite of Jackson James' fans. She freely admits this was because she used to walk around with her shirt off. I'm just thankful all that footage belongs to Jackson and he doesn't show it anymore because watching it makes it clear that he's gotten really, really old.

And then, at the ripe old age of twenty-one, Mom found herself kicked out of the castle and two months pregnant. Seven months later, I came along and was given a name "designed" to prove the truth. There was a paternity test, and a court hearing, and Jackson's famous "Why didn't anyone get me a picture of the baby?" line right before the trial was supposed to begin.

There wasn't a trial after that—I guess looking at someone who's got your hair and eyes makes it sort of hard to say, "Hey, she isn't mine"—and although Mom's never told me the details of what happened, I know he acknowledged that he was my father and offered her money, which she turned down. She said she didn't want to owe him anything. She just wanted him to be my father.

And he was. For a while, anyway. One of my earliest memories is visiting him at the castle and how huge and magical it seemed. It stayed that way as I got older, was a place where I could do anything I wanted. Stay up all night? Jackson didn't mind. Eat ice cream for dinner? Jackson had people who would bring me a big bowl on a silver tray. There were toys, there was a pool, there was a huge backyard full of girls who always wanted to braid my hair or tell me how pretty I was. Until I was five, and started school, I honestly thought most women walked around without their shirts on.

I loved the pets that lived there too, the dogs and cats that Jackson bought for the girls, animals who ate well and were walked by the staff but were never really noticed by their owners except for quick pats on the head when the girl who once wanted them was in the mood.

I spent hours with them, and they used to follow me wherever I went. For years, Jackson kept a picture of tiny little-girl me on his desk, smiling and waving at the camera as I played on the lawn, a mass of dogs and cats around me.

I don't know if he still has it or not—one of Jackson's many "quirks" is that he doesn't like to throw things away, so I'll bet it's archived in a box somewhere—but the thing about that picture is that it shows exactly what I was to Jackson.

I wasn't a person to him, not really. I was more like just another pet. Adored when needed for the cameras, or if he wanted to prove that he was still young enough to be a dad, or if he was in the mood to act like he cared about "family"—and never thought about the rest of the time.

I found that out when José died.

I visited Jackson for the last time just after the funeral, and it was the last time I saw him. The last time I called him Dad.

I never should have called him that. He never deserved it, and if it hadn't been for José, I wouldn't have known what it was like to have a real father and a real family. José showed me love isn't about getting whatever you want, but about being there—really being there—for your family. Love is about little things, like being told to put on your seat belt when you get in the car, or a kiss on your forehead as you pass through the room. A gentle squeeze of your hand when you're crying after hearing that everything you know is going to end.

I don't know if I can do that. Feel that kind of emotion anymore, I mean. Since José died, I want to get out of Slaterville. I worry about Mom. I want Josh. But that's it. I can't connect it all together. I feel like I'm pieces of a person instead of the real thing.

I don't really think Josh is my soul mate. I want him to be, but he isn't. He's too good, too caring. He is all the things I want to be, and I can't help but dream that if I can somehow get him to like me, I can learn to be like him.

I want to be happy, to fall in love—to be real—but I know, from Mom, that it's so much to ask for. Too much, maybe.

ten

Something's up when I get to school. I know because people are looking at me, and that doesn't usually happen.

I check my outfit, but it's okay. Old, loose jeans that I've had forever, and a gray knit shirt that I gave José on his last birthday. He didn't live long enough to wear it. The cuffs have holes in them from where the knit has started to fray, and over the years, the color has faded from a dark slate to pale smoke, but I'll never get rid of it.

My hair is in its usual ponytail, and I've even remembered to put in the styling goop that keeps it in place and makes my hair look a little darker.

So everything's the same, but still, people are looking, and as I'm heading to first period, Brent passes me, humming some song

I guess I'm supposed to know, and says, "What you got on under that shirt, Hannah?"

"Boils," I say, and spend a second watching him try to figure out what I mean before moving on. Ass.

In gym, I sit next to Michelle. This year she and I have this class and chemistry together, and we always end up as partners on any—and every—project. Sometimes I want to tell her I'm sorry she's cursed with having Jameson as a last name, but I've never actually said it. I'm not sure if she'd laugh or not.

Gym isn't really gym at Slaterville. It's half class, half occasional exercise. The whole thing was off the schedule for years, actually, until a bunch of parents who were worried we were all going to get fat complained, so now we have an extra period every day. As if we don't spend enough time in school already.

Right now we're "studying" nutrition, which means that instead of being sent outside to run back and forth until class is over—or until the teacher gets distracted by something shiny—we sit around discussing such fascinating topics as "why junk food is bad."

The fact that there are snack machines about ten feet away from the classroom door makes this extra amusing.

"So, have you thought of four ways to eat more vegetables?" Michelle says.

"Nope. You?"

"Nope." She grins.

I grin back and wonder why she even talks to me.

See, Michelle isn't a freak or anything. She's a cute girl. You know the kind I mean. She isn't pretty, not really, but she clearly gets up early every morning and makes the most of what she's got. She smiles a lot, is nice to everyone, and, as a result, is one of those rare people who can talk to almost anyone and have them talk back.

"So, okay, what about this whole putting carrots in spaghetti sauce thing?" she says, and then wrinkles her nose at her textbook. "Ugh, forget it, I just don't care about any of this."

"I know. You'd think they could teach us something useful like—I don't know. What to do if you're asked to put carrots in spaghetti sauce."

She grins. "Or how to drive. I'm still on the waiting list for driver's ed, and last week I found out I might have to wait until next year to take it. Next year! I'm never going to get my license."

"You can take one of those outside classes."

"My parents won't let me," she says, making a face and twisting a silver ring around her left ring finger. "They say they don't want to pay for it, but I know they just don't want me driving. They're so annoying."

"Yeah," I say, although I'm pretty sure my definition of an annoying parent is very different than hers.

Her ring pops off her finger and lands on my desk. When I pick it up and hand it back to her, I notice there's something engraved inside.

"Thanks," she says, snatching it back and flushing a little. "I bet you think it's stupid, right?"

"Your ring?" I say, confused. "Why would I think that?" I don't wear any jewelry, it's true, but I don't think it's stupid. I just don't own any.

"Oh," Michelle says, and then smiles, turning the ring so I

can make out the word engraved inside. *Wait.* "I signed the pledge at church ages ago, but the promise ring came just last week. I don't want to tell my parents it's too big because I don't want them to think I don't want to wear it."

"Right," I say. "That's really nice. The ring, I mean. And everything else. Too bad I can't have—"

Shit. Shit shit shit. Michelle's eyes have widened—just a little bit—and now I know I have to say something to fix this. And fix it really fast.

"I mean, I could get one if I wanted because I—um . . . you know. But my mom would never go for it. She thinks people who do the whole 'promise to wait' thing are fooling themselves and should learn about sex instead of . . ." I am so NOT helping myself here. "I—I think the ring looks really nice on you."

"Sure," Michelle says, her face red, and I can see people around us watching, wondering what I've done to make Michelle—so nice! so cute!—upset. "I'm . . . I'm going to get a bathroom pass."

And then she gathers up her stuff and leaves.

If I was a more hopeful person, I would have thought there was no way the day could get any worse, but I'm not hopeful. I know the day will get worse.

And it does.

I finally find out—via Brent, again, in the hall before last period—why people have been looking at me. Jackson, in his infinite jackassery, has mentioned me in the weekly online promo for his stupid show. The clip has made the rounds because one of his girls has an accidental nipple slip, and naturally everyone wants to see that.

And before the nipple pops out, Jackson apparently says I'm going to come "party" with him, because in Jackson's world that's what you do with the 17-year-old daughter you haven't seen in years.

And then his girls "interrupt" and tell him it's time for bed and basically, I suspect that by the time the nipple popped out it sounded like I was headed up to see Jackson and spend the weekend doing all of New York, especially since Brent told me Jackson closed by saying, "For highlights of my previous trips to the city, be sure to check out the archives and see just how well I took a bite out of the Big Apple. Here's hoping my daughter can keep up with me!"

Brent does a great impression of Jackson, but standing there watching him leer his way through Jackson's little speech, punctuating it with comments about Jackson's "girls" sucks.

I don't leave, though. I don't even try to. Guys like Brent want me to walk away, want to chase after me and see me upset, so I just stand there staring at his forehead and waiting for him to finish. And when he finally does, when he's exhausted all his "jokes" and says, "So, tell me exactly how you're going to keep up," that's when I can react.

So I do. I smile at him, sliding my hands out like I want to hold his or hold him. (Eww, but necessary.) He grins, and his buddies make stupid horny guy noises, and I take his hands. Then I grab his thumbs and bend them backward as far as I can.

He yelps and has to work to twist away, causing his buddies to laugh, and him to counter with some shouted suggestions for them (and me) to suck his dick.

I ignore him, but turn back to look when he gets cut off mid-rant, surprised that something's shut him up, and see that Finn has wandered by and somehow managed to knock Brent into a locker.

He's hit him pretty hard too, so hard I can see Brent doing that head duck/grimace thing guys do when they're trying not to scream in pain.

"I never heard Finn was good at football, but I guess he does okay when it's guys on his own team," someone says.

Someone who sounds like Josh.

My heart starts to pound, and I turn around, happily looking away from Brent, who's rubbing his head and complaining as Finn shrugs, his fists clenched, and see Josh.

Let me repeat that.

I see Josh.

Josh is here. Josh is talking to me.

Josh has never spoken to me in school.

"Hi," I say. I know I should say something else, something better, something smart and funny and perfect, but I can't. Josh is talking to me. And smiling. And his hair is falling into his eyes and he's so gorgeous and so concerned-looking, like he's seen the whole thing and decided to rush to my rescue.

"I heard Brent. 'Stupid' is too good a word for him. He didn't hurt you or anything, did he?"

I wish Josh hadn't heard anything Brent said, but the shame of it pales because he cares. I mean, he wants to make sure I'm okay. Plus, he thinks Brent is stupid. (This is less of a big deal, though, because most everyone thinks that.)

"I'm fine," I say. "I'm used to him."

"Yeah, some people are just—"

"Hey, Hannah, way to go with the thumb thing," Finn says as he walks by. "And Josh, way to stand there and watch, man."

"At least he said something," I say. "Asked if I was okay."

"Hey, I saw what you did to Brent's thumbs," Finn says, stopping to look at me. "I know you can take care of yourself."

"Bye," I say with as much force as I can, hoping he'll get the hint and move on. When he doesn't, I add, "I wouldn't want you to be late to class. Or have someone else end up a victim of your outstanding walking skills."

"Yeah, well, Brent's a big guy and the hall was crowded," Finn says, shrugging. "I think I can manage to avoid knocking you over, though."

"Hey, Hannah, I gotta go," Josh says as one of his activist girl friends—who I can tell wants to be a girlfriend—comes by and puts her hand on his arm.

I wish I could put a hand on his arm.

He glances at Finn, then at me. "See you around."

I wave, even though the girl friend who wants to be his girl-friend is whispering in his ear and he isn't looking at me anymore, and then sigh myself off to class.

I'm so depressed by the conversation-that-wasn't-really-one with Josh that I stop by the mall to see Teagan on my way to work, but she isn't interested in talking about what I should have said to him. Instead, she wants to talk about Finn.

"You do realize he did that on purpose, right?"

"What, butted in on my conversation with Josh? Yes. He does

it all the time at work because he gets bored, and in Government he's always—"

"No, not that," Teagan says. "Hannah, it's obvious that he knocked Brent into the locker so he'd shut up."

"Please. Finn didn't knock Brent down because of what he'd said. He came up to me afterward and told me I'd done a good job taking care of myself. Does that sound like he was looking out for me?"

"It sounds like he thinks you can take care of yourself but wanted to bash Brent's head in anyway. God, I wish someone would bash somebody's head in for me."

"You did not just say that."

"You know what I mean," Teagan says. "I wish someone wanted to, you know, look out for me."

"I can give Finn your number."

"I don't think it's my number he wants."

"First, whatever, you're crazy. Second, he actually has my number because we have to have them posted at work in case of an emergency. And third, you're crazy."

"You already said that."

"I thought it was worth repeating," I say, and she swats my arm as we say good-bye and I head to work.

Finn hitting Brent on purpose? Yeah, okay. Sure. Teagan is so . . . well, wrong. I mean, I love Teagan, I do, but she wasn't there.

And even if—even if she is right, I want Josh.

Josh, who is sweet and wonderful and perfect. And who talked to me. At school!

eleven

And if Teagan was with me when I walk into work, I could so show her why Josh is perfect. And why a certain other person isn't.

Finn is slouched in his chair, stuffing cheese puffs in his mouth. And not just one or two. I swear he has half the bag in there.

"It helps if you chew," I say, and he swallows, then shakes the bag at me.

"It's all air and fake cheese. Chewing would slow me down."

"I don't see how you can eat that stuff," Josh says to Finn, and I look at him—he's not inhaling cheese puffs, of course—as I sit down.

I hope I'm not being too obvious, but how can I not stare? And how can Josh look so good just sitting there? I think it's his hair. It's so dark and curly and clearly not styled into place or anything. It's like he doesn't care about how it looks, but it's still perfect.

As I watch, he unwraps one of those natural food bars, the ones made from oats and fruit and wild grains and stuff.

"This is the kind of thing everyone should—hold on, I've got an order," he says.

He looks down at his terminal and I slide into my chair and put on my own headset. BurgerTown and its hordes of hungry customers wait. Sigh. Maybe I can finish up whatever orders are waiting real fast and then look at Josh some more.

Maybe I'll even be able to work up the nerve to talk to him.

No such luck, because apparently every person who lives near a BurgerTown has decided they have to visit the drive-thru. After a couple of hours, I'm still taking orders, my throat is as dry as sandpaper, and I don't ever want to hear or say the word "burger" again.

Also, I'm starving. At some point, Finn shoved his bag of cheese puffs at me and I ate the rest of them, covering my headset so that people giving their orders wouldn't hear me crunching away.

Finn nudges my foot as I say, "Thank you, and drive up to the first window, please," for what feels like the ten millionth time, and when I look at him he points at a piece of paper lying between us.

"Sorry about what Brent said before," it says.

It's sweet. Even if it does have bits of cheese puff around one edge.

"Thanks," I say. "But, um—look, why are you even friends with him?"

Finn blushes. "We aren't really. We're just—we're on the team together, and back when I first moved here, he really went out of his way to—"

"Beat you up?"

"No," Finn says, still blushing. "Look, we don't hang out that much anymore, and if you thought I agreed with what he was saying, I didn't. Don't."

"Don't those negatives cancel each other out?"

Finn grins at me.

"You—do you want—?" he says, but Josh cuts him off.

"Orders," he says, sounding pissed, and Finn sighs dramatically and says, "Oh, right, those things. Thanks for pointing out what my job is, man."

I grin before I can stop myself—sometimes Finn can be pretty funny—and then see Josh frowning at Finn. And me. I shove Finn's piece of paper away and get back to work.

I can be the right kind of girl for Josh. I can, and I will.

But then Finn shoves the piece of paper back at me a few orders later and he's got a tic-tac-toe board all sketched out, and when I put one hand over my headset microphone and whisper, "Do I look like I have time for this?" he puts a hand over his microphone and says, "You're just afraid I'll kick your ass like I did last time."

"Am not!" I say, and the guy who's giving me his order says, "What?"

"Sorry," I say, and make "ffzzzting" noises. "Technical difficulties."

And then I play tic-tac-toe with Finn. I win three games. Finn wins two. Josh sighs a lot, and I feel bad because I'm not taking orders as fast as I could—but I still play.

See what I mean about Josh being a good person? He doesn't do stuff like this, doesn't play games at work. I shouldn't either, but I can only hear people say, "Well, I think I want the number two meal. No, wait, the number six. No, hold on . . ." so many times before I have to do something to keep myself from screaming, "I don't care! Just order!"

Things finally slow down around 9:30, and the three of us sit slumped in our seats discussing who had the biggest order. The winner gets to leave early.

"Four jumbo combos and six lemon pies," Finn says. "Do you ever wonder what's in those things?"

"Nope," I say. "That way lies nightmares. Also, fourteen cheeseburgers with no pickles, extra mayo, extra mustard, and only the top part of the bun."

Finn whistles. "Point for annoyance and volume. I think you—"

"Four jumbo combos, three regular combos, two light and healthy meals, one chicken sandwich, ten onion rings, and all the drinks had to have no ice," Josh says. "In one order. Plus I got to hear all about how it was for a marketing team meeting that had gone on for six hours. I win."

"I don't know, man," Finn says. "You gotta give points for ordering so many cheeseburgers at one time, not to mention the creative way in which they were requested."

"Oh, come on, I had to hear marketing talk," Josh says, smiling at me. "You know I win, right, Hannah?"

I nod, mesmerized by his smile. And by how he's looking right at me. Maybe I should ask him if he wants to go get coffee sometime.

Yes, I should do it, especially since he's still looking at me.

Okay, I'll do it right—

"Great, I'm out of here," Josh says, and stands up, tossing his bag over his shoulder. "Better luck next time, guys. Oh, and hey, Hannah, about that stuff with your dad—"

"My dad?" I say, thinking about José and wondering how Josh knows about him. And then I realize who he means. "You mean Jackson?" Why is Josh asking about Jackson?

"Yeah. I just—I think it's really amazing that you have a father who . . . he just sounded really happy about seeing you. Or at least that's what I heard he sounded like. I didn't actually see the clip."

"I bet," Finn mutters.

"I just . . ." Josh leans in toward me. "I wish my dad was like yours. I wish he wanted to spend time with me, but instead all he does is work and talk about how he wants to make sure there's enough money for me to go to college and crap like that. I bet Jackson's not like that. I think it's cool you call him that, by the way."

"Josh, man, if you want to get out of here, you better go now because I just saw Greg dragging his ass out of his office to talk to the night shift."

"Okay, thanks," Josh says to Finn, and then looks back at me. "See you around, Hannah."

"Bye," I say, and weirdly, I'm not sorry to see him go. I don't like talking about Jackson, and I don't get why Josh wanted to. It's also weird Josh thinks I'm somehow lucky compared to him. If only he knew how Jackson really was.

"What are you doing over there?" Finn says, nudging my foot. "Falling asleep?"

"Sort of," I say around the big Jackson-created lump in my throat. "So Greg left his office? Is the building on fire or what?"

"Nah, Greg's still where he always is. I just figured Josh was so hot to win and get out of here that he might as well go. Plus the last thing I want to hear is another poor Josh story. Oh, the agonies of having it all!"

"Hey, did you—?" I start to ask, wondering if Finn somehow knew that I didn't want to talk about Jackson, and then break off because . . . well, how would he know that?

"Did I what?" Finn says.

"Did you bring anything else to eat?"

"Not for you," he says, but then gives me half a turkey sandwich he made "for the ride home."

"Thanks," I tell him as we're walking out to the parking lot and he looks at me for a long moment, so long that my heart starts to pound all crazily and I think he's going to do something or say something, but he just says, "You should have won for those cheeseburgers, you know," and then asks me if I'm sure the crap-bucket will start.

Teagan is running late, and when she gets out of work she's

silent, which means something bad happened. Teagan only ever stops talking when something's wrong.

"What is it?" I ask as we turn onto her street.

"I got offered a promotion. Assistant manager."

"And?"

"And what?"

"And that's bad how?" I say.

"It's not exactly bad," she says. "I mean, the pay is pretty crappy, but it's better than what I'm making now. It's just that when I heard the offer . . . I don't know. It just hit me that this is it. This is what I do. I work at Jeans Hut."

"Well, just for now. You're going back to New York."

"I don't know if I am. Just thinking about trying to find another place to live, and a job, and going to school again . . ." Teagan sighs. "I just . . . I feel like my life is over."

"Come on, your life isn't over. You take the job for six months, save your money, and then leave. I mean, going back to school is, what, filling out a few forms? That's not so bad. And I know you can find a place—"

"Okay, no more talk about my crap job or school, please. Instead, let's talk about something fun. Tell me all about Josh and what he said to you tonight."

"Teagan."

"Hey, you have to allow me to live vicariously. You've seen a picture of the guy I spent my high school years hooking up with, and Ted was . . . well, you saw the picture."

"There's nothing to tell. It was really busy, and Josh had the strangest order, so he got to leave early."

"He had the strangest order? What was it? Twenty-seven milkshakes with no lids and two straws each like you had that one time?"

"How do you remember stuff like that?"

"I fold clothes all day. What else have I got to remember? Now, what was the order?"

I tell her, and she makes a face. "What's so strange about that? What was your weirdest order tonight?"

As soon as I'm done talking, she says, "Hannah, you won that contest! He cheated you out of your win!"

"Okay, calm down there, crazy woman. It's not like I lost a fortune or anything, and Josh's order was pretty weird. Plus he took more orders than anyone else."

"How do you know he took more orders?"

I shrug.

"He told you," she says, grinning. "So, what did you and Finn do now?"

"What does that mean?"

"Oh, come on," Teagan says. "If Josh was taking most of the orders that means you two had to be doing something. And Finn did defend your honor earlier."

"You didn't really just say that."

"Still not hearing what you were doing."

"It was nothing. We played tic-tac-toe for a while. You know we do that sometimes."

"Oh, I know," Teagan says.

"Okay, how did you make that sound like we were rolling around ripping off each other's clothes?"

"Interesting that your mind immediately went there."

"You're insane. You know that, right?"

"I sell jeans for a living. Of course I'm insane. What else happened?"

"Josh asked about Jackson."

Teagan is silent for a moment.

"He doesn't seem to know you very well," she finally says. "You hate talking about Jackson. What did Finn say when he asked about Jackson?"

"He didn't."

"Huh," Teagan says. "What did he do when Josh asked?"

"Nothing really," I say as I pull to a stop in front of her house. "Well, he sort of told Josh to go ahead and leave."

"Hmm," Teagan says, and gets out of the truck.

"What do all these h-noises mean?"

She grins at me. "You know what they mean. I know you know what they mean. The thing I don't get is, how come the idea of Finn liking you scares you so much?"

"Scares me? Ha! You know what? I think *you* like Finn."

"Uh huh."

"Okay, going now."

"Okay," she says, still smiling.

I stick my tongue out at her before I drive off. I don't think about what she said, because it's insane, but I do wonder why Finn didn't bring up Jackson. And why Josh did.

Don't get me wrong, I still like Josh—how could I not?—but maybe he isn't perfect.

Then I remember how he's brought me food and made me a

CD. And what he looks like. And, just to show I'm not shallow, I also haven't forgotten that he believes in things and writes poetry.

I do talk to Finn a lot, though, don't I? But then, it's hard not to, because Finn talks a lot.

Grrr. Teagan! I can't wait to get home and relax.

twelve

But I can't relax when I get home, because when I walk in, Mom's eating macaroni and cheese.

Also, she's wearing clothes.

"What's wrong?" I say, because hello, clothes. Also, Mom never cooks unless she's really upset, and even then she only cooks two things: boxed macaroni and cheese or grilled cheese sandwiches. José used to say Mom married him just for his cooking, and then grin at her until she'd kiss him.

"My server's down," she says, and I nod while I help myself to the rest of what's left in the pot. It's a little burnt, but it's still warm and cheesy and good.

"What else?" I say when I sit down next to her at the kitchen table.

"No server means no site. And that equals no money."

"Come on, Mom. You could have gone to the backup site and done your show there." She made this deal with some computer guys a while ago where they get a free site membership and she has a backup server, complete with a place she can go and do a chat if she needs to. So far it's only happened once, when Mrs. Howard decided to "fix" her front lawn and "accidentally" knocked out our Internet service.

"Okay, there's something else too," she says, and gestures at a white envelope lying on top of our never-dwindling stack of bills.

"What is it? Something with the mortgage?"

"No," she says, shoveling in another mouthful of macaroni and cheese, and I know what's happened.

"Jackson sent something," I say, and Mom nods once, tightly.

"It's plane tickets, right? Don't worry, I'm not going to see him," I tell her, and she shakes her head.

"It's . . . there was a card for me inside," she says, her mouth trembling, and I get up and get the envelope.

Inside the envelope are train tickets to New York, leaving this Friday and coming back the same day. So much for Jackson flying me in. Or listening to me.

Or really wanting to see me. A one-day trip. One day, solely for the cameras. Solely for his show.

I knew it, of course, but seeing the proof . . . forget it. I already know how he is. I put the tickets down and look for the card.

"I can't find it. Did you—?" I say, and break off, because

Mom starts to cry. Really cry too, the kind of crying that sounds like a heart breaking.

I haven't seen her cry since José died.

"Mom?" I say, my voice rising into a little-girl squeak, like we've both been sucked back in time.

"I threw it away," she says, fighting back tears. "Burned it over the sink, in fact. He . . . Fran wrote he hoped I was doing well, and that he thought the site looked fantastic. You know the kind of stuff he says. But at the bottom of the note Jackson actually wrote something, and he—"

She pauses and takes a deep breath. "He wrote that he hoped . . . he said he hoped José was well, and congratulated us on being together for so long. Like he doesn't know that . . ."

That ass. That stupid, old ass.

"He forgot," I tell her. "He's old, Mom, really old, and Fran clearly didn't read what he wrote before she put it in the envelope."

"That's just it," she says, wiping her nose on her sleeve like a little kid. "I can't even be mad at him. He's always forgotten things—birthdays, names—you know that. But just thinking about what could have been . . . it would have been eleven years, Hannah. We could still be in Queens, in our little house, and I could still be—"

She starts crying again, and I go over to her and kneel down next to her, putting my arms around her.

Happy. That's what she was going to say. She could still be happy.

Like she used to be.

thirteen

I help her to bed, finding tissues so she can blow
her nose, turning back the covers and telling her to sleep, that
tomorrow will be better.

"It won't," she says as she closes her eyes. "It never is."

She says it so quietly and so wearily that my own eyes start
to burn.

I say goodnight and go before I can start crying myself,
bawling for what might have been, for a life in Queens with
José and Mom. I go downstairs and wash the dishes, check her
e-mail to make sure she sent a service request to her site-hosting
service, and then open the hall closet, the one Mom never even
looks at.

She pretends it away because all of José's things are in here. All that's left of the life we once had is here, in this tiny space. I touch one of his shirts. They used to smell like him.

Now they don't smell like anything.

I still like being around José's things, though. I can't really remember what his face looks like without a photograph anymore, can't remember how he smelled, but at least I have his shirts and pictures. I like knowing that part of José—a real part, something I can touch and not what people say will always be with you, memories or the spirit or whatever—is here. Is real.

Mom met José when I was six. I don't remember it, but then I wasn't there.

We were living out in LA, back when she was filming what would end up being the last five episodes of *Cowboy Dad*, and her car broke down on her way to pick me up from after school day care.

She tried calling everyone she knew to see if someone would get me, but it was the end of the day and everyone was stuck in traffic themselves, or just didn't bother to answer their phones.

José was the tow truck driver who showed up an hour and a half after she called, and after the Happy Child Day Care people had informed her that they didn't tolerate lateness more than three times and she would have to find someone else to watch me.

José used to love to tell the story of how he and Mom met, and to this day I can still remember exactly how it went. Some kids like to have fairy tales read to them at night, but I never wanted that when I was little. I had a real happily ever after story to hear.

"Well," he'd say, "there I am, in my truck, thinking about how much I want to move back to New York, when I see your mother. She's standing by her car, yelling at all the people going by who are yelling at her for being stuck—and she is furious. I take one look at her and that's it. That, I know, is the most beautiful woman I'll ever see."

"And then what happened?" I'd ask.

"Well," José would say, "I go up to this beautiful woman, and when she sees me she points a finger at me and says that I'm late, that her little girl is waiting for her, and what am I going to do to fix things?"

"Marry her," I'd say, and José would smile at me.

"That's right. 'I'll marry you,' I said, and she just looked at me and said, 'Be serious.' And I said, 'I am.'"

"And then she looked at you for real," I'd say.

"That's right," José would tell me. "She looked at me for real and saw I was serious. She saw I knew she was for me like you know that tomorrow morning the sun will rise."

"And then what happened?"

"Well, then I looked at her car, told her it wasn't going anywhere, and offered to take her to get you."

"And she said no."

José would nod. "So I said, 'You take my truck. I'll wait here. Just come back and get me when you're done.'"

"And then she came and got me."

"Right. She came and got you and took you home."

"And me and Nancy ate eggs for dinner," I'd say. Nancy was my mother's roommate back then, another struggling actress who ended up working for a cruise line. We still get postcards from her once in a while, always from somewhere in the Bahamas. "And when I woke up, you and Mom were in Vegas."

José would nod. "She came back to give me my truck, and when she did, I had to kiss her, and then—" He'd clap his hands together. "Boom! We knew we were going to get married."

"And then you did."

"And then we did," he'd say. "And now we all live here, in Queens, forever and ever." And then he'd kiss my forehead and turn to look at Mom. She always came in as he finished the story, and stood smiling at him and me, a big, happy smile like the sun was shining inside her.

José got sick when I was twelve. At first he said it was nothing, even though his brown skin looked almost gray from the pain of the headaches he was getting, and when he gave Mom the star he'd bought her to celebrate their anniversary, they couldn't drive out of the city to see it because he didn't feel well enough to go.

When Mom finally got him to go to the doctor, it turned out all the headaches were from a tumor. It was too large and too advanced for anything to be done, and José checked himself out of the hospital and came home. He lay in bed, telling me stories when I got home from school, teasing my mother until she'd smile whenever it looked like she might cry.

It took three months for him to die and Mom had to see

it. Had to watch it all, knowing there was nothing she could do. I remember his hands, clenched and thin against the bedsheets, his closed eyes when the pain was very bad and he was waiting for his pills—and toward the end an IV—to kick in.

At the time I thought those moments when he was able to open his eyes and look at us meant he might get better, even though he told me he wouldn't. I just . . . I had hope, back then. I didn't think things would ever change.

The morning he died, I showed him the new barrettes I was wearing. I wore my hair down then.

"Almost as pretty as you are," he said. "Come kiss me good-bye."

"Good morning, you mean," I said, because I kissed him good morning, good afternoon, and goodnight every day.

"Good morning," he said with a smile. "I see the sunshine in your hair."

When I got home from school, he was dead. He had no family, except for a few cousins in Arizona. They came for the memorial service, and I think they were surprised he'd married a white woman, that the little girl he'd called his daughter clearly wasn't his at all. They looked long and hard at us, at Mom with her face full of tears, and we never heard from them again.

Mom did nothing for weeks after he died. She'd get up, send me to school, and then go back to bed. When I came home she'd get up, talk to me in a dull, washed-out voice for a moment, and then disappear back into her room. I honestly think she didn't want to live. But she did.

She lived, and eventually she started to make plans. I saw Jackson once after José died, the last time I ever saw him, and he didn't mention what had happened. He didn't say he was sad or even that he was sorry. He didn't say anything about José at all.

I told her that when I got home, and said I never wanted to see him again.

"Well, then there's no reason to stay here, is there?" she said, and soon after that another family bought our house and we loaded everything into the car and left. We drove straight down the East Coast until one night on the interstate we passed a man in a tow truck talking to a woman whose car was broken down on the side of the road.

"We're here," Mom said, and got off at the next exit.

And that's how we came to Slaterville. Not because Mom wanted to be here, but because for just a moment, she saw something that reminded her of José. That reminded her of the life she'd had.

Mom believes in signs like that. If she didn't, she never would have married José. But looking into the closet, at his clothes and his tools and the sheets from the bed he and Mom shared, the one he died in, I wish she could have seen other things as well.

I wish she could have seen how sick José was. I wish she'd made him go to the doctor sooner. I wish she hadn't believed in him and their forever so much because losing him—she still doesn't talk about it. It's like there was her life with Jackson, some time in LA, and then a blank spot until we got here.

And then I go to bed, because José was right about one thing. The sun will rise tomorrow. It always does, and all the wishing in the world for the way things were, or for what they could have been, won't change that. It won't change how things are.

fourteen

Mom seems fine in the morning. She's up and exercising when I roll out of bed, just like always, and when I ask her how she's feeling for the fifth time, she sighs and says, "Hannah, it's okay to be sad sometimes. You know that, right?"

"Yes, fine, I get it," I say, exasperated because I'm not going to get anything more from her than that—other than watching her do leg lifts—and leave.

I end up getting to school late anyway, though, because the crapbucket doesn't want to start.

The day only gets worse from there. Michelle doesn't say hi to me like she usually does in gym, and in desperation, I say the one thing I used to dream people would say to me back when we first moved here and school was a nightmare.

"I'm sorry," I say. "About yesterday and your ring, I mean. I like it, and I like the idea behind it. And it looks nice on you too."

"Oh," Michelle says. "Thanks." She shifts a little in her chair. "So, can I ask you something?"

"Sure." Is she going to ask me if I'm a virgin? I don't want to talk about sex because even though I've never done anything with anybody—I haven't even been kissed—the fact that Mom does what she does, and that Jackson is who he is, matters more than anything I might say. Or not do.

"How come you always wear your hair like that?"

"Huh?" Not what I was expecting.

"It's just . . . well, I'd love to have your color hair," Michelle says, and twists a lock of her gorgeous (and normal-colored) brown hair between her fingers. "I mean, I put highlights in mine, but it's still blah." She leans closer. "Don't you want to do something other than stuff it in a ponytail?"

I shake my head. "I'm no good with the whole . . ." I gesture at my hair. "Yours always looks nice. Mine is just . . . I'd look stupid with it down."

"No, you wouldn't."

"I would, trust me."

She raises her hand and tells our teacher that she has to pick up something for the junior class fund-raiser. "And can Hannah come help me?" she asks. "All those jelly beans are really heavy."

Our teacher grunts something that must be a yes, because I find myself in the hall, being guided by Michelle into the nearest bathroom.

"Jelly beans?" I ask.

"There's something like 5,000 in a big glass jar and the idea is people pay three bucks to vote and whoever is closest wins the jelly beans and a trip to the beach that Addison's mom donated. It's stupid because the trip can't take place over spring break or in the summer so nobody's going to want to go and . . ."

She keeps talking, and I wish I had her life. I wish I cared about jelly beans and could talk about anything—and to anyone—so easily.

Inside the bathroom, she steers me to the sinks, and before I can stop her, she's pulled my ponytail holder out. Surprisingly, it doesn't hurt when she does it. I always manage to pull out a couple (okay, many) strands of hair.

I see myself with my hair down, of course. At home, at night and in the morning, but I don't usually look at it.

It's so long, down to almost the middle of my back. I don't remember the last time I had it cut.

"Oh," Michelle says kind of sadly as my hair doesn't spring into curls or artfully arrange itself around my face.

"Told you," I say, and start gathering it up.

"I guess I just thought it would look like your mom's, with the curls and stuff. Only blond, you know?" Michelle says.

"Nope, no curls," I say. "Your hair is actually more like hers than mine is."

"Really?" Michelle sounds both horrified and intrigued.

"Yeah. Did you ever see *Cowboy Dad*? Your hair looks a lot like hers did back then."

"My older brother loved that show. My dad got him the

DVDs for his birthday and we all had to watch an episode. It was . . ." She trails off.

"Terrible," I tell her. "I tried to watch the DVDs once. I made it four minutes into the first episode, where Cowboy Dad says, 'Yee-haw!' and the laugh track goes off for what seems like ten hours."

"I know!" she says. "I mean, how is that funny? Not that— I'm sure your mom was good."

"She looked good," I say. "Or at least, she looked like how hot women were supposed to look back then. But anyway, you could totally get your hair to look like hers did, with the curls and all." She probably couldn't. Mom's *Cowboy Dad* hair was the prod-uct of extensions and people following her around and styling her to perfection.

"You think?"

"Sure." She could at least come a lot closer than I would.

The bell rings, and she waves at me, then disappears into the hall. I duck into a stall and pull my hair back again, then head to my next class. And I admit, for about ten seconds when I get to lunch, I have this idea that maybe Michelle will wave me over and ask me to sit with her, but what happens is I walk in, and then walk right back out.

I end up eating in the media center, surrounded by ancient computers that groan as they load the portal to the few sites the school allows us to visit.

After school, I go to the mall to see Teagan. She's talking a customer through proper jean sizing, which is how Jeans Hut gets their customers. What they do, according to Teagan, is make every size bigger than it should be, which means that Mom, who wears a size two, finds that a size zero is too big for her. I always send her to Jeans Hut when she's worrying that she looks fat.

"What's up?" Teagan asks when the woman she's waiting on has gone to try on a size eight, grinning because Teagan has sworn that the size ten, "Would just fall right off you!"

"Nothing."

"Same here," she says, and then looks more closely at me. "Wait a minute. Something happened. Tell meeeeeee."

"I took my hair out of the ponytail today."

"Liar."

"I did! Well, sort of. This girl, Michelle, said I should wear my hair down. Or did until she took the ponytail holder out."

Teagan pretends to stagger back a step. "You actually spoke to someone? You?"

"Hey, you went to school there. You remember how it is."

"I do," Teagan says. "But I had friends. Granted, I don't talk to them anymore, because they all have real lives in places that aren't here, but still."

"I have friends," I say, stung. "You're my friend."

"You can have more than one friend. Or so I've heard."

"Teagan."

"All right, I'm just saying," she says. "So, this hair girl, Michelle, you talked to her and . . ."

"Well, see," I say, and then tell her about the whole chastity ring thing.

"Oh," Teagan says.

"Exactly. So you can see why we're probably not going to be hanging out all the time."

"I don't think it's that bad, though. I mean, she talked to you today, right?"

"Yeah, but—"

"Fine, continue with the 'I'm all alone' routine."

"I don't have a routine, and I'm not alone. I just don't have much in common with anyone at school."

"So alone!" she says, grinning.

"That's it, I'm going to work," I say, and bump her shoulder with mine. "See what you've reduced me to? Going to work early."

"So start talking to Michelle, and then you can bitch about me to her," Teagan says, and then bumps my shoulder back. "Look, Hannah, I think you aren't as alone as you think you are, okay? I think you're just scared."

"Scared?"

"You heard me."

"Whatever," I mutter. "You know I hate it when you're earnest."

"Yeah, yeah, go on," she says. "And hey, after work I want an update on the Josh thing. A real update. Like a you-bought-him-coffee update."

"You'll hear all kinds of stuff," I say, grinning, and head off, telling myself I'm not going to work early and that I'm finally (finally!) ready to make my move.

fifteen

I'm not.

I can't bring myself to stop and buy Josh coffee—*again*—and so I do end up at work early, where my options are to sit in the crapbucket and pretend I'm not sitting in the parking lot waiting to go to work (I might as well tattoo "Hi, I have no life" on my forehead) or go to work and wait in the break room for the current shift to finish.

I pick the break room, where I can sit alone without anyone possibly seeing me sitting alone. Like, say, Josh when he gets to work. Plus since I haven't actually started work yet, I won't lose any pay, and . . . well, that's about all sitting in here has got going for it. The room itself is as depressing as ever, cinderblock walls, beat-up chair, hideous fuzzy orange sofa with Finn—

With Finn lying on it, reading a thick book with one of those "I'm a classic!" covers. (You know the ones I mean—they've all got dark backgrounds with a picture of an old woman or flowers or something. Never anything good.)

"Are you reading?" I say. It's not that I don't think Finn can read or anything, but it's just—well, not what I expected to see. I figured Finn spent his spare time doing whatever it is guys who aren't Josh do when they aren't in school. Burping, or something.

"Try not to look so surprised," Finn says. "I read. I can count to ten. Sometimes I can even write my own name."

"I've seen your handwriting, so I'm not sure about that last one."

"Funny," he says, and puts the book down. "What are you doing here?"

"Getting ready for work. Why are you sitting in here reading . . . ?" I peer at the cover. "*The Brothers Karamazov*? The book we talked about the other day? That's what Josh is reading! Why are you reading it?"

"Well, it's what happens when you're in the same English class."

"You aren't in his class," I say, and then realize what I've given away.

Finn laughs, damn him. "Wow, you stalker. I didn't know you had it in you. But there is more than one section of Accelerated English, you know."

"I know," I say, and I did know, sort of. I know Slaterville has a bunch of accelerated classes, part of some program that has something to do with college credits, and I know Josh takes two,

English and Foundation of Thought, which Teagan tells me is a fancy way of saying "philosophy."

I had no idea Finn was in anything accelerated, though.

"Seventh period," Finn says. "If you decide you want to stalk me."

"I see enough of you already," I say, and knock his feet off the sofa so I can sit down. "How come Josh doesn't know you're taking AE too?"

"Well, I keep waiting for him to bring it up during our daily chats . . ." He puts his feet on my lap. "Me and your boyfriend don't hang out, obviously."

"He's not my anything."

"You wish he was, though," Finn says. "Right?"

"So you, what, sneak to work early and do your homework?" I tap his feet, and when he won't move them, shove them off my lap. "Wait, are you hiding your genius from the world so your friends won't make fun of you?"

"Yes, that's it exactly," he says. "You know how it is with guys like me. The minute you can spell words of more than two syllables, you get beaten up for liking book learning and such."

"Ooooh, sarcasm. Now I know you must be super smart."

"Pot, meet kettle," he says with a grin, and sits up. "See how perfect we are together?"

"Oh, quit it," I say. "I just didn't think you were the kind of guy who . . . you know. You don't talk about being in an accelerated class."

"What am I supposed to say?"

"I don't know," I say, thinking of Josh and how I always

know what's going on with his homework because he brings it up at least once a shift. "I'd be running around waving those fifty-pound books in people's faces, that's for sure."

"No, you wouldn't," he says. "You never talk about yourself. I didn't even know you could talk until you started working here, and even then it took a while to get you to say anything."

"You didn't even know who I was until I started working here."

"How do you know?"

I laugh, but it comes out weirdly shaky, almost breathless. "Okay, you've had your eye on me since you moved to town in ninth grade. Better?"

He looks at me then, and I feel that same strange pull I've felt around him before. That same weird and alarming sensation where I notice Finn. Like, really notice him.

"All right, I don't want to bother you when you're reading," I say, feeling a little freaked out, and get up. "See you at work."

"Hannah," he says, and I think about looking back at him—and I mean, really think about it. Think about what might happen if I did.

But I don't. I just walk out to my truck and tell myself that whatever I felt in the break room was probably the result of fumes from that ancient—and hideous—sofa.

I see Josh pull into the parking lot, and immediately slide down so he can't see me. I should get out and try to walk in with him, but . . . well, I don't want to rush things. I want to get to know him. I'm taking my time, that's all.

I like that idea much better than Teagan's scared theory, that's for sure.

Now if I could just get myself to believe it, I'd be all set.

But I am scared about Josh. Not of him, because he could never hurt anyone. I can tell that by just looking at him, and when I finally walk into work and see him sitting at his terminal, his dark hair falling over his forehead, I know I'm scared because I—well, why would someone like him want someone like me? And thinking about that—facing it—sucks.

"Hey," Josh says, looking up and smiling at me. He gestures at a pile of books he's got spread out on the floor. "You wouldn't believe how much homework I've got."

"Sorry," I say, and sit down in front of my monitor. Then I try to think of something else to say. Why is talking to him so hard? Should it be this hard?

I wish I knew more about this stuff. But aside from Teagan, who have I got to ask? Nobody. (Although, strangely, I do think about Finn for a second.)

And speaking of Finn, when he comes in, he sits down and looks at me. His blond hair has little bits of sofa fuzz in it. I smile at that, and his eyes widen for a moment before he smiles back and whispers, "What's up?"

"Your hair," I tell him, and lean over to brush the orange bits out of it.

"Oh. Thanks," he says, and then looks at Josh.

"So, Josh, me and Hannah were talking about love before," he says, and I stare at him.

What is he doing?

"Really?" Josh says, not sounding very interested, and my heart sinks to my ankles.

"Yeah. Hannah doesn't believe in it, but I think it's possible."

"You don't believe in love?" Josh says, looking at me. "Not at all?" He sounds interested now.

"I believe in love," I say.

"Okay, then name someone you love," Finn says. "I dare you."

I'm going to murder him.

"My mom," I say through gritted teeth, and then look at Josh. "Sorry. Finn's just being . . . well, himself."

"No, it's great," Josh says. "I was actually talking about this with Micah yesterday, because she and I don't agree on what love is at all. I think it's about freedom and being who you are, and she thinks it's this really restrictive thing, where you have to be with only one person." He looks down at his feet. "We sort of had a huge fight about it, and she said I'm not the one for her."

He's not with Micah anymore? Wow. WOW. Okay, I have to say something, and let's try for something good.

"I'm sorry." Oh, excellent. Grade A material there, Hannah, really.

"Thanks," he says, and looks up, a shy smile on his face.

He's smiling!

He's not with Micah!

He's smiling at me!

"So she dumped you?" Finn says. "That's rough, man. Is that why I saw you with that friend of hers, Peyton, the other day?"

"We were talking about Micah, yeah," Josh says, and he and Finn look at each other for a second before Finn shakes his head and says, "Guess you won't have to buy Micah a birthday gift now, huh?"

"Finn, he just got dumped—I mean, broken up with. I mean—sorry," I say to Josh, and make a face at Finn as I ask him, "How do you know when Micah's birthday is, anyway?"

"She's in my English class," Finn says. "Sits next to me. And you said I never talk about school."

Josh sighs and I turn back to him. "Are you all right?"

Josh tries to shrug, but ends up looking all broken and sad. I know this is terrible, but he looks amazing when he's miserable. He also looks like he needs someone to help put him back together, and I so want that someone to be me.

"I'm still getting her a gift," he says to me, like Finn isn't even in the room. "She's still in my heart, and the best gifts come from there."

"You don't mean that literally, right?" Finn says. "Because I don't think anyone wants an actual heart. Or anything that's inside it."

"He means something like a poem, ass," I snap, and Finn blinks at me, then turns bright red.

"I'm thinking of a song, actually," Josh says. "I've been writing a bunch lately for my band." He leans in close, which is nice, but a song? He writes songs?

I am so not interested in musicians. A lot of old ones hang around Jackson, and they seem to think singing some song people listened to when dinosaurs walked the earth means they should get laid forever and ever.

"Or, maybe I'll have a tree planted in her name," Josh says. "Something really meaningful. Something that helps others."

"Like a star," I say, thinking of Mom's face when José gave

her one. When he got really sick toward the end, she put up glow-in-the-dark stars on the ceiling so they could both "see" it.

Josh grins. "You mean those certificates that say a star is named after you? Micah loves making fun of that kind of cheesy stuff. Thanks, Hannah."

"She wasn't kidding," Finn says quietly, and I say, "Shut up, of course I was," as evenly as I can, and watch Josh smile at me.

But the thing is, Finn's right. I wasn't kidding.

sixteen

Luckily, demand for burgers is insane like always and we're all pretty much busy after that. Josh focuses on work like always, and although I really like that about him, I sort of wish he wanted to keep talking to me.

But instead I'm stuck with Finn, who asks me things like "How much fish do you think is actually in the fish sandwich?" and so on. Surprisingly, by the time we're done debating that, as well as whether or not the fact that there's no milk in BurgerTown's "Iced Cream" means it should be called "Moo What?" or "Name That Chemical Cream," it's time for my break.

I dig all the change I can find out of my pockets and then sit in my truck eating a package of fig cookies. As I'm finishing the last one, Finn knocks on my window.

I sigh and open the door. "I'm coming back to work, all right? I didn't think I was gone that long, but—"

"It's not that," Finn says. "Greg's looking for you."

I stare at him. Greg never looks for anyone. Greg never leaves his office.

"I know," Finn says. "Come on."

We head inside and almost run into Greg, who is pacing by the door.

"I found her," Finn says. "She was outside looking at the terminal . . . uh . . . junction. We thought it might be acting up."

What the hell is he talking about? I glance at him and he widens his eyes at me, a go-with-it look.

"Oh, right," I say, remembering I'm supposed to be punched out if I'm on "break," even if that break is just me eating cookies in the crapbucket.

"Good, good," Greg says. "Those junctions are important. Anyway, the thing is . . ."

I wait, but he doesn't finish his sentence.

"The thing is . . . ?" Finn says.

"The phone call," Greg says, and then blinks, red-eyed, at me. "Your dad called. Wants you to call him."

"My dad?" I say, but Greg doesn't answer, is already ambling back to his office.

"He said that your . . . he said that Jackson called," Finn says.

"Right," I say, trying to sound like I'm not freaked out, but I am. Jackson called me? Jackson called me here? I mean, I know he knows where I work because Fran knows, but still.

Jackson called me?

"Hey," Finn says, cupping a hand under my arm. "You okay?"

"I . . . yes," I say, and try not to lean into him. I want to, though. "I guess I need to call Jackson. Can I use your cell?"

Finn shakes his head. "I mean, you could, if I had it, but I left it in my jeans the other day and my mom washed it so I sort of don't have one right now."

"Hey, you can use the phone in here," Josh says, sticking his head out into the hallway. When Finn looks at him, he says, "I could tell something was going on."

"I don't think I'm supposed to use that phone," I tell Josh. "It's for calls to tech support and stuff. But . . . ?" Why is it harder to ask Josh this than it was Finn? "Do you have a cell phone I can use? I can pay you back for the call if it'll cost you—"

"My battery's dead," Josh says. "I forgot to charge it last night. Just go ahead and use the phone in here. If anyone asks, we'll say Polly was making calls, right, Finn?"

"Sure," Finn says, and then leans toward me. "You sure you're okay?"

"Fine," I say, even though I'm not. I really don't want to call Jackson, especially in front of other people. But he called here, at work. He called me.

He's never called me.

What if something's happened to him?

"Come on," Josh says, and then he takes my hand and walks me to the phone. His hand is cool, and his fingers are long, twine easily around mine. He squeezes once, gently, before he lets go, and then sort of stands there.

"I'm okay," I say, and he nods and moves away.

I dial, and look around as the phone rings. Finn's back at his terminal, taking orders, and Josh is too. But it's like he knows I'm looking at him because he's looking at me, and when our eyes meet, he smiles, as if he's trying to give me courage.

He's so sweet. If all guys were like him, the world would be so much better.

And then someone picks up the phone.

It's Fran.

"Hi," I say cautiously, and she says, "Hannah, hello! How are you?"

"Um, fine. I . . ." I glance around again, but Finn is still working and Josh is sort of looking at me . . . no, wishful thinking. He's looking at his terminal. His chair is just a little closer to me than usual. "I got a message that Jackson called. Is he—?"

"Dammit," she yells, which was not what I was expecting. "Ron, you pin-weasel, I told you to call Hannah at home. H-O-M-E. I'm sorry, Hannah, I did ask Ron to call you, but since he's an idiot, he screwed it up."

I hear the sounds of someone—male, and certainly Ron—apologizing, but Fran keeps talking. "Well, now that you've called, Hannah, I do know Jackson wants to speak to you."

"So he's okay?"

"Of course."

He's fine. He didn't call. I can't believe I thought he did. That he would.

I am so stupid.

"I should go. I'm at work and—"

"Is this my lovely daughter?" Jackson says, suddenly there

on the phone. "How are you? I can't wait to see you in New York." And then he laughs and says, "Oh, me too, Hannah."

Unbelievable. He's being filmed for the show. He didn't call, he's fine, he's the same.

He's exactly the same.

I take a deep breath. "I—you know what? I'm not coming to see you, and you and your stupid camera crew can go—"

He hangs up. Just like that, I hear a click, the sounds of the cameras moving away, and then Fran is back on the line saying, "Hannah," all sadly.

"Don't," I say. "I just—don't. And I'm not allowed to get personal calls at work, so don't call here again."

I start to hang up and then Jackson says, "Hannah, wait," and I freeze.

He shouldn't still be on the phone. I heard him hang up. Plus there's no clicking in the background now, no sound of cameras rolling. Why is he talking to me?

"I really do want to see you," he says. "Did you get the train tickets?"

"Why are you acting like you want to—?" I break off as I remember I'm not alone. That I've already said an awful lot, more than anyone, even Teagan, has ever heard me say about Jackson, and I've been talking to him.

I am talking to him.

I look around again. Finn isn't looking at me, but Josh is. He's smiling, like he's encouraging me, but I don't want encouragement. I just want to forget I actually thought Jackson would ever call me.

"I haven't seen you in almost five years, Hannah. I miss you. You're my little girl and I . . ."

He keeps talking, but I can't hear him. I'm too angry. I'm so angry I'm shaking.

This is what he has to say? This?

Does he really think I'd believe that he missed me? That he could ever miss me?

"Stop," I say, biting the word out. "Just—you pushed way past the bounds of believability by the second sentence, and I'm not coming to see you tomorrow or any other time. Fran, what's really going on?"

Jackson clears his throat, and then I hear another click. He's hung up. Again.

Figures.

I don't know why my eyes are stinging. I blink hard to make them stop.

"He does want to see you," Fran says, coming on the line once more. "I'm sure you know he mentioned your visit in the show promo."

"Yes, I heard all about it, thanks."

"You should be proud to be his daughter," Fran says softly. "He's a man who's created an empire. A whole world that's being showcased on a television show—"

"And?" I say, cutting her off.

"And ratings are down," she says, and this is why I like Fran. She yells a lot, but she doesn't bullshit. "The producers think having you on the show will draw in younger viewers."

"So it's all about him, as usual."

"It's not that simple."

"Of course it is," I say, and hang up, slamming the phone down so hard it makes a satisfying cracking noise. Jackson is simple because everything, in his mind, is about him. Always has been, always will be.

And I was stupid enough to think he wanted to talk to me. That he'd actually called me. Idiot! I take a deep breath, trying to calm down, and turn around.

Josh is right behind me.

"Oh," I say, and he hugs me. Just wraps his arms around me and pulls me in close.

Josh is hugging me.

But here's the thing: It doesn't feel amazing. It doesn't even feel good. I actually want to be alone right now, but I can't because I'm at work.

"I'm sure things will work out for you and your dad," he says, and I push away from him.

"It's Jackson, okay?"

"Oh, sorry," Josh says. "How come you don't call him Dad?"

"Hey, I've got a ton of orders over here," Finn says, and I'm glad to be able to just shrug at Josh and get back to work. I'm even glad to be taking orders, glad to hear people ask for extra pickles or no mayo or demand to know what our french fries are made of.

Well, maybe not so much on that last one.

After I deal with the french fry person—I didn't think anyone thought they were made of anything other than potatoes—something hits me in the forehead.

"Ow," I say as whatever has hit me falls into my lap. I look down and see a candy bar.

"Brain food," Finn says before he takes another order, and I inhale the candy bar. I don't care what doctors say, chocolate can make things better.

"Thanks," I tell him when I get a chance, and for a second, when he smiles at me, I think that Finn is . . . I don't know. Something. He's easy to talk to. And he's not perfect, but he did get me chocolate. Chocolate without mint in it, even.

But then Josh says, "Hannah?"

I look at him, and he says, "Can we talk? Later, I mean."

Oh. OH.

I nod.

And then I wait, nervous and impatient—and actually a little scared—for our shift to end. When it finally does, Josh pulls me aside.

"Hey, about before, I just . . . I wanted to say that I think . . . well, I think you're pretty special," he says, kind of stumbling over the words a little, like he's hesitant to say them, and now I wish he'd hug me again. And then kiss me.

But he doesn't. He just waves and walks off.

I sigh.

"Hannah, I just . . . I want you to know that if I pause a lot when I tell you how special you are it's because I want you to think I'm . . . very . . . very . . . deep," Finn says.

"Wow, thanks. Nice to know you're sure no one could actually think I'm special."

"That's not what I said."

"Yes, it is."

"No, it's not," he says.

"Is."

"Isn't."

"Fine. I'm leaving now," I say.

"Hey, Hannah?"

"What?"

"You're—I mean, I think you—you kick major phone ass," Finn says, blushing again.

"Okaaaaay," I say, like he's being weird, but I actually like what he said. I like the idea that I kicked Jackson's ass. Even if it was over the phone.

seventeen

"What happened?" Teagan says as soon as I pick her up.

"Jackson." I take a deep breath. "He called me at work. Well, actually some assistant who probably got fired did, but I ended up calling back and it sucked. A lot. The call only happened because ratings for Jackson's stupid show are down, but then Jackson came on and started doing this 'Oh, I want to see you' thing. And when I told him no, he hung up on me."

"Oh, Hannah, I'm sorry," Teagan says. "That really sucks, and—wait, how did you call him back? Did you finally get a cell and not tell me?"

"Nope, and this is where things get really craptastic. I had to call from work. Like, from the room where I sit. With Josh and Finn around."

"Why?"

"What do you mean, why? Finn managed to wash his phone, and Josh's battery was dead."

"But what about a pay phone? Or asking Greg?"

"A pay phone? Are you kidding me? We're lucky we have two vending machines that usually work and a semi-clean bathroom. BurgerTown isn't big on atmosphere."

Teagan puts her feet up on the dashboard. "Greg would have let you use his phone."

"Yeah, maybe, but I didn't think about that. I thought . . . when Greg told me about the call, I thought Jackson . . . I thought maybe something had happened to him. And then, when he actually talked to me, I thought that—I thought he wanted to." I listen to the crapbucket creak as we turn a corner. "I feel plenty stupid about it now, though."

"You're not stupid. He is your . . . you know. Father."

"Yeah, but biological only and he didn't even want to believe that for a while."

"I really am sorry," Teagan says again, and taps her feet against the dashboard. "What about Josh? Did anything happen with him?"

I look over at her, grateful, and smile. "Are you trying to change the subject?"

"Obviously," she says, smiling back. "So . . . what happened with Josh?"

I shrug.

"Oh, come on! That's no answer!"

So I tell her about the gift conversation.

"I wouldn't mind getting a star from a guy," she says. "I don't think it's cheesy."

"Me either," I say, thinking of Mom and José. "But hey, he also gave me a hug after I talked to Jackson."

Teagan's silent.

"A hug," I say again. "That's pretty big, right?"

"Maybe if you sounded like you were happy about it."

"I am."

"Wow, monotone enthusiasm. Huge!"

"I am!" I say again. "Is that better? It was just . . . I'd just talked to Jackson. I wasn't in the best mood."

We turn onto her street and Teagan taps her feet against the dashboard again as we stop by her house. "Don't get mad at me for what I'm going to say, okay?"

"Oh, goody, I can't wait to hear this."

"Look, Hannah, you've liked Josh for a while now, but you never do anything about it. I mean, you work with him, and he talks to you, but yet you still never—"

"I'm not his type," I say. "I see the girls he's with, and they are so not me that it's—"

"Yeah, but he's talking to you. He's buying you stuff. Does he have to tell you he loves you before you'll say, 'Hey, want to go out sometime?'"

"I—look, I want to do that. I want to be that kind of person. Ask him out. Talk to him without freezing up. But I keep thinking that if we do go out, what if I . . . ?"

"What?"

I shift in my seat. "I'm Jackson James' daughter, all right? And all he thinks about is sex. So if me and Josh are alone . . ."

Teagan laughs.

A lot.

"Thanks," I say, and reach over, knocking her feet off the dashboard. "Really, now I feel great."

"I'm sorry, Hannah," she says, still giggling. "It's just here you are, worrying that you're some kind of nympho to the point where you won't do anything, and would Jackson even think about stuff like that? Or is he too busy trying to pick up chicks?"

"'Pick up chicks'? Fabulous outdated slang there."

"You do see what I'm saying though, right?"

I shrug.

"Is that a maybe?"

"Maybe," I mutter.

"So then will you please just ask Josh out?"

I tap the steering wheel with one hand. "I—okay."

"For real?"

I nod.

"Good," she says, and waves before she heads inside. I can tell she thinks I won't do it, but I will. I even practice what I'm going to say as I drive home.

But when I get home, the phone is ringing.

And when I pick it up, it's Jackson.

eighteen

"Hannah," he says, not a question—he recognizes
my voice—but I won't let that get to me. It doesn't matter that this
is the first time he's ever called me. I won't say anything.

After a moment, he says, "I'm sorry about before," and I
listen for the telltale sounds of people filming and listening to
his every move, including this call.

I don't hear anything, and I don't understand why.

"Where are the cameras and the sound guys? Standing by
waiting for your signal to zoom in for a shot of you pretending to
care about stuff?"

"You're my daughter. Not stuff. And I do care."

He sounds like he means it. But then, Jackson always
sounds like he means what he says, because he does mean it
when he says it.

He just doesn't mean it for longer than it takes to say it.

"Seriously, where's the show crew?"

"I'm in bed," he says. "There's no cameras here. At least, not ones from the show."

Ugh. I wait for the giggles from his "girls," but again, there's nothing.

"Are you . . . are you alone?" Jackson's never alone, unless he's doing something he really loves, like archiving all the photos that have ever been on his site. He can spend hours organizing them, and has each one put into a special folder that he then puts into a scrapbook. (That's right, Jackson likes to make scrapbooks. Some party animal, huh?)

"I am," he says. "I know Fran spoke to you about the situation, but I want to ask you—"

"I'm not coming to New York to be filmed as some sort of ratings stunt. The last time I saw you, the producers made it look like I showed up, had a meltdown, and then had to be sent home. And you let them do that. You let them do that when you could have stopped them."

"Don't be upset with me," he says. "I can't—you know I can't bear that. And this trip isn't about the show. There won't be any cameras. It's just for one day, and I want it to be just you and me. I miss you. It's been five years, Hannah."

"And whose choice was that?"

He clears his throat and I wait for the inevitable hang up.

It doesn't happen.

"I want to see you," he says again. "You're my only child, and I miss the way things used to be. I miss how you used to run

117

around the castle, how we'd eat ice cream and watch movies. And the parties? Remember those? You'd get so excited about the costumes I'd order for you . . ."

"I was a little kid then," I say. "I was stupid enough to believe you when you said you'd always be there for me." To my horror, my voice cracks on the last words.

"I want to make it up to you," Jackson says. "I want to make up for all our lost time. I want you to come to New York."

"Make it up to me? After five years, you think one day can fix things?"

"I think it's a start, and I want to try. I don't . . . is it so hard for you to believe I want to see you? That I want to see my own flesh and blood?" His voice goes quivery, like an old man's.

Like he is. An old man, surrounded by people who will do anything he wants but who leave without looking back when he says it's time.

He's not stupid. He knows people use him just like he uses them, and if there's one thing about Jackson that makes me feel sorry for him, it's that. I think a huge part of why he liked having me around when I was little is that he didn't have to do anything for me. He didn't have to buy me cars, or plastic surgery, or jewelry. I just liked being with him.

I used to love going to see him. I used to love him.

"Please," he says, and I've never heard him say that before. It sounds wrong, strange, but as soon as he says it, I'm powerful, I've done what nobody else has. I've made him ask for something.

I've made him ask for me.

"No cameras when I show up? No cameras at all?"

"Nothing but you and me," he says. "Just say you'll be on that train and I'll—Hannah, I'll be so happy."

And that's when I know I'll go. When he says that, when I hear how surprised he sounds by his own emotions. When I hear he really will be happy to see me. When I can tell that I do mean something to him.

"All right," I say, "I'll come," and he says, "Hannah, thank you," with so much joy in his voice that I'm a little girl again, standing in my father's castle and feeling like there's nowhere else I could ever want to be.

nineteen

I'm not supposed to interrupt Mom when she's working—as if I want to be seen on camera at candymadison.net— but I know I need to tell her about tomorrow and Jackson. I write a note and slip it under the den door.

She's out in the hall about five seconds later.

"You're going to see him?" She doesn't sound mad, just startled. "Are you—what happened?"

"He called me."

She crosses her arms over her chest. "Really?" I hear surprise, and something almost like envy, in her voice.

I nod.

"Oh," she says, and I can't tell what she's thinking from that one word. Is she upset?

I guess she isn't, because she says, "Do you need a ride to the train station in the morning?"

"No, I'll just take the truck."

"Okay. I guess I'll get back to work."

"That's it?" I say, surprised. "I haven't seen him in five years, you cry when the tickets come, but when I say I'm going, you don't care?"

She sighs. "I wasn't upset about the tickets and you know that. Also, you're old enough to make your own choices."

"Okay, so you were upset about José. I miss him too, Mom, you know. We can always talk about that, about him. I mean, he was—"

"Stop," she says, her voice sharp, and goes back into the den, shutting the door behind her.

I slip another two notes under the door, asking her to come back out and talk to me, but she doesn't, and I finally give up and go to my room.

The phone rings again as I'm getting into bed. It's Teagan, and she's crying.

"What's wrong?" I say, worried because Teagan doesn't cry. At least, I've never seen her cry.

"My parents said my mother's finally well enough for me to go back to New York."

"Isn't that—isn't that good?"

She's silent for a long time. A long, long time.

"Teagan?" I say.

"I—I didn't drop out of school to come home," she says,

low-voiced. "I flunked out. I can't go back. And I never told—my parents don't know that."

I'm silent for a moment, shocked. Teagan flunked out of school? "Oh. Okay. Well . . . what about somewhere else? There's got to be other schools in the city—"

"No," she says. "I just—I couldn't handle it if I flunked out again."

"That would never happen. I've seen your stuff, you know, and it's amazing."

"I—hold on a second."

I hear muffled voices, and then she comes back on and says, "My father just came in and told me he's going to bed. Which means I have to be in bed because that's how things are around here. I'm sorry, I gotta go."

"But—"

"Sorry," she says again, and we say goodnight. I stay up for a while, worrying about Teagan and wondering if I should call her back even though her dad will get upset, but right when I lie down and try to fall asleep, the phone rings once more.

"I knew you'd call back," I tell her. "So, okay, there's got to be tons of schools in New York, and if you want, I bet I could go by them and pick up forms or something. Whatever you need."

A voice that most definitely isn't Teagan's says, "Um, Hannah?"

A guy's voice.

A guy is calling me.

Josh?

Oh please, let it be him. He did see how upset I was

tonight, after all, and it would be just like him to—

"Hannah?" he says again.

"Yes. I mean, hi."

Oh, good job, Hannah. Way to sound like an idiot.

"Hey, it's Finn. I know it's late, but I was just wondering—"

Finn? "Finn?"

"Yeah."

"Oh. I thought you were someone else."

"I figured that one out already," he says. "So . . . you're going to New York?"

"Yeah." I wait for him to ask about Jackson, but he just says, "Oh. Well, um, anyway, I know it's late and you've clearly got stuff going on, but I—" He clears his throat. "Well, I . . . I just wondered what we're supposed to do for Government."

"You're calling me to ask about homework?"

"Okay, no," he says, his voice sounding kind of shaky. "Look, I've been thinking about stuff, and I just wanted to tell you that I . . ."

And that's it. He falls silent. I wait a moment, but he still doesn't say anything.

"Well?" I finally say, and for some reason my hands are sweating and my insides are all weirdly fluttery.

"Your truck sounds like it needs to have the belts checked. I know you hate it when I tell you stuff like that, but there, I said it," he says, the words tumbling out in a rush. "Bye."

And then he hangs up.

I glance at the phone and then hang up too, shaking my head. Guys are so weird.

twenty

Mom wakes me up in the morning.

"I want to drive you to the train station," she says.

And then she does, but doesn't say a word the whole way there.

What's going on?

"Mom, are you all right?" I say as she pulls into the parking lot.

She laughs, but it sounds like a sob. "No."

"Is it—is it Jackson? Me going to see him?"

"No."

"Then what's wrong?" I think about last night. About what happened when the tickets came. "Is it José?"

She nods. It's a tiny movement, but I see it.

I smooth my hands across the knees of my jeans, nervous

because she and I don't talk about this, about José. Angry because we don't talk about him, because whenever his name comes up, she finds a way to change the subject, goes back to work or suddenly has something to do. She always says she's sad but fine, just fine.

She makes me feel bad for wanting to remember him.

"I know the card upset you, but is it my fault you won't look at his things? That we have his stuff in a closet and you pretend it's not there? That you hardly ever talk about him or how things were? I mean, Mom, I miss him, and it's . . . it's hard for me too."

She stares at me. "Hannah, you don't know . . . you don't know how hard it is. I have to live without him. Every day, I wake up and think that. And every day, I get up anyway." She shakes her head. "I can't even think about José without wanting to cry, and I don't like to talk about him because I'm still trying to deal with living without him."

Oh. I knew she missed him, but I didn't know it was like this. I didn't know her pain was still so raw. I'm so used to seeing Candy Madison, barely dressed and smiling, always smiling, that I forgot who she really is. I forgot she's a person. That she's Mom.

"I didn't—I'm sorry," I say. "I didn't know it was so hard and I—I didn't know."

"You'll miss your train," she says gently, kissing my cheek, and when I hesitate, she leans over and opens the car door for me. "Go on."

As the train leaves, I see her standing by the fence that separates the parking lot from the train tracks, scanning the windows. I tap against mine but she doesn't seem to notice.

But she stands there, watching, until the train is gone.

I think about Mom and José, and how I need to remember that Mom is someone real, and that Candy Madison isn't her, not all of her, until New York starts to come into view and the people around me shift in their seats, getting ready to move. Looking like they can't wait to arrive.

And then I'm there, in the city, getting off the train and walking up into the station.

I've always known Slaterville is one of those places you pass on the highway that looks like everywhere else, that there's nothing special about it, but I hadn't realized how slow it is. Everyone in the station, with the exception of people like me, moves like they have somewhere to be, and they have to be there now.

And Jackson isn't here.

I try to ignore the small but miserable voice that starts howling inside me, one that's wailing at the unfairness of it all, of Jackson letting me down again. Of Jackson not loving me. I try to push away what's left of the little girl who once thought she was a princess, but it's hard.

Five years, and I still haven't managed to get rid of her.

And then I see an enormous guy, so tall he doesn't seem human, holding a sign that says HANNAH.

I walk over to him slowly, and when I'm halfway there he says, "Hannah?"

"That's me," I say. "I guess Jackson sent you. One of his girlfriends' breasts spring a leak or something?"

The guy doesn't even crack a smile. "Mr. James is outside," he says. "Come with me, please."

"Right," I say, and he does grin at me then, all business and teeth, and passes me a tiny cell phone, one I've seen pictures of stars using in *Celeb Weekly*.

"You're here," Jackson says, and through the phone, his voice is so warm, so happy. "I'm right outside, waiting. Didn't want to cause a commotion in the train station."

"Oh," I say, and then the guy takes the phone back. I follow him outside, wondering if anyone would even notice Jackson here, in this sea of people all trying to get somewhere else, and then I see the limo.

It's huge, an enormous SUV painted Jackson's favorite shade of blue. (The color of his eyes, of course.) It's preposterous-looking, but there are no cameras or camera crews around it, and when I get inside, all I see is Jackson.

"Thank you, Darryl," he says, and the big guy who walked me out turns around from what seems like miles away, up in the front seat, and nods. "Anything else, Mr. James?"

"No, thank you."

Darryl nods again, and one of those privacy screens, all dark glass, slides up, leaving me alone with Jackson. I look out the window. Every street is so crowded.

"It's good to see you," he says. "I've missed you."

I look at him. He's dressed in his usual jeans and blue silk shirt, his hair carefully combed to hide the fact that it's thinning in the front. And the sides. And the back.

He looks smaller than I remember too, not shorter exactly, but almost like he's shrunk somehow, and his clothes hang loosely on him.

127

He looks like what he is, an old man, and for some reason my eyes sting a little, my throat squeezing. I shake my head to stop it.

"You look lovely, Hannah," he says. "More and more like your mother every day."

I don't see how that's possible, given that we don't have the same color hair or eyes or anything else that I don't keep covered by my usual huge shirt and jeans, but I shrug. "Thanks. She's doing fine, by the way. Nice of you to ask."

"I know she's fine. We link to her site from mine, and I hear she's getting quite a bit of traffic. And that she looks as wonderful as ever." He leans forward, looking at me intently, so intently I can't look away.

"It's been too long. You've grown up, and I've missed it. I've thought about you every day, though. Wondered how you were, what you were doing."

I'd forgotten how he sounds. How he focuses on you like no one else exists, how he makes you feel like you're his whole world.

I force myself to take a deep breath. "You're right. It's been a while since I've seen you."

"Five years," he says. "Five years and three months next week, in fact. I wish you'd come out to visit me. You still have a room in the castle, you know, and that will never change."

Now my eyes sting again. "Really?"

"Of course. You're always welcome. You know that."

"Then why . . . why wouldn't you let me stay with you?"

The one thing Mom doesn't know—and won't ever know—is the real reason why I stopped talking to Jackson after José died. It wasn't because Jackson didn't say anything about José.

It's because I asked Jackson if I could live with him, and he said no.

twenty-one

The last time I saw Jackson was a few months after José died. I went to visit him at the castle, an early birthday present, and I was happy Jackson remembered I was turning thirteen soon. He tended to forget birthdays.

Going to the castle was like going to another world, as always. Everyone was happy to see me, and Jackson said it had been too long, that he missed me, and that he wished I could stay longer. And me, stupid me, thought I could escape the sadness that had wrapped around me and Mom, thought I could live in the castle and play the part of Jackson's little princess forever.

So I asked if I could stay.

He had Fran tell me no. He couldn't do it himself, wasn't

even in the castle when she told me. He stayed away until right before I left.

That's how and why the footage of 12-year-old me screaming at him ended up on his show. It's why people talked about me at school when we first got to Slaterville, the bolder ones asking me why I screamed that he'd never been a real father, asking why I said I wished he'd died instead of José. They also wanted to know who José was.

The meaner ones just said I was crazy, and snickered about Jackson's lack of reaction. ("Poor kid," he'd said to the camera, and the next scene showed him dancing with his girlfriends at a club, smiling like he didn't care about anything at all. And he didn't, did he? At least, not about me.)

"I couldn't let you stay because of your mother," he says now, as if it explains everything. "I had to think about her."

"Sure you did. Except Mom didn't even know I asked, Jackson. So I know she didn't tell you to say no. You chose to say it. You didn't want me living with you."

He clears his throat, looking uncomfortable, and I wait for him to tell me he has to call Fran or pretend he has to ask Darryl something. Anything to stop talking to me.

But instead he looks right at me.

"I said no because she would have let you move in with me," he says.

I knew it. I mean, he's never said that he told me no because he knew I'd move in and he didn't want that, but I knew it anyway.

Still, finally hearing it doesn't feel so great. Parents are supposed to want you, aren't they? Even if it's just for weekend visits? But Jackson didn't even push for that after my last visit. He just . . . disappeared. I went home, me and Mom moved to Slaterville—and I never heard from him.

I made a mistake coming here.

"Take me back to the train station," I say, and I'm proud of how I sound. My voice is calm and steady. I sound like I don't care.

"That's not—" He clears his throat again, and I stare at the faint scars on the sides of his face, lines showing that he's had his skin drawn up, tightened. At least Mom hasn't had surgery like that to make herself look younger.

At least Mom wants me.

"She would have said yes," he says, "but then she would have been all alone. And Candy—she needs people around her. People who love her. She needed—and still needs—you. And besides, you're the best thing in her life. She's always told me that."

"Right, because you two talk so often."

"We used to," he says. "We were together for over two years, you know. And Candy's been through a lot."

"Two whole years? Wow. And I'm stunned to learn that Mom's been through a lot. Oh, wait—wasn't a lot of that because of you?"

"Hannah," he says, and pats my knee, just like he used to when I was little. "I didn't say no when you asked to move in to hurt you. I did it because I thought it was the right thing to do. And I was so upset that you got upset that I—"

"Didn't bother to contact me for five years?"

"Didn't know how to talk to you," he says. "Don't you

think—?" He clears his throat. "I hated seeing you so upset. I hated seeing you cry. But I didn't want you to hate your mother. I wanted you to—"

"Stop," I say. "I get it. You did it all for her, made yourself into the bad guy to be noble, and gosh, you're sorry I was so upset and it just broke your heart to see it. But I saw the show, Jackson. I saw how you felt so bad that you said, 'poor kid,' and then went to a club and acted perfectly normal. For you, anyway."

Jackson laughs.

He actually laughs, like all this is funny, like I've just told a joke or something, and I hate him. I wish I hadn't ever wanted to live with him.

I wish I'd never thought he was anything at all.

"Hannah," he says, and moves so he's sitting next to me, putting an arm around my shoulder, "that was on the television show. It wasn't real. You know that."

"Oh, so someone who looked like you said 'poor kid,' and then went out and had fun and made sure to talk about how much fun you were having?"

"You know what I mean," he says. "You're a smart girl. After you left, I went to my office to be alone, and didn't come out for—well, I needed to be alone. But then I had to get back to work. I wasn't even talking about you when I said 'poor kid.' I was talking about a girl who wanted to be on the site and wasn't ever going to make it. But the show used it, and you know how they change things around. I didn't—I never meant to hurt you, Princess. I love you."

I look at him, and I can see he's fighting tears.

I look out the window, my own eyes burning. No one but Jackson has ever called me Princess, and no one has told me they loved me in so long. Mom does, I know, but she stopped saying the word after José died, like it had become cursed.

"I know I hurt you, though," he continues, his voice still tear-filled, "and I swear I'm going to make it up to you. Okay? I've turned off all my phones, left instructions I'm off-limits to everyone, and now it's you and me."

I look at him.

"Just like old times," he says. "Well, except that now you're probably too old to want to eat ice cream for lunch. Wait, hold on a minute." He pretends to hold a magnifying glass, and peers at me. "Was that a smile I saw? Just for a second?"

I'd forgotten how incredibly goofy he can be. How unafraid he is to be silly just to make you smile.

"Aha!" he says. "There it is for real. Prettiest smile in the whole world, that's for sure."

"Right, Dad," I say, and then we both sort of freeze. I haven't called Jackson Dad since the last time I saw him.

"Thank you, Hannah," he says, openly crying now, and kisses the top of my head. I can feel his tears, wet against my hair. "Thank you for giving me this chance."

We drive through the city for a while, and Jackson points out places to me. I look at some of them, but mostly I look at all the people. I can't see Teagan here, even though she was. Everyone's moving so fast and looks so assured, or at least in a hurry, and Teagan doesn't do or look any of those things.

"And here we are," Jackson says, looking out the right window as the limo starts to slow down.

I look out the window too, and see a regular-looking restaurant. And then I see a waitress pass by with an enormous chocolate thing, towers and towers of it drizzled with chocolate sauce and topped with whipped cream.

I hope I'm not drooling. I look over at Jackson, and he's smiling.

"I know my Princess," he says. "Let's go inside."

twenty-two

We do go in, but the restaurant is so crowded
that we end up standing just inside the door. Ahead of us, two
girls are talking about their wait.

"Do you want to stay?" one girl says.

"Do you?"

"It'll be over an hour. We could go do something else."

"Yeah, but then we won't get to have that," the other girl
says, pointing at a passing waiter and a large piece of what looks
like extra-chocolate chocolate cake.

I try not to drool and then Darryl is pushing through the
crowd, taking Jackson and me up to the front of the line, where a
pretty but frazzled-looking hostess blinks at us. She doesn't recognize Jackson's name when Darryl says it—she's only a few years

older than me, and doesn't look like an actress/model wannabe, but instead has the funky vibe of an artist, right down to the patchouli smell.

"I'm sorry, but I don't have anything open—" she says, and is then cut off as an older, very well-dressed man comes out of the back.

"Thalia, this is the man I told you about this morning," he says, shooting a brief and embarrassed look at Jackson. "Remember?"

"Oh. Right. Sorry. I didn't realize you were so ol . . . I mean, let me lead you to your table, Mr. Jackson."

"Old," she was going to say. Old. I can tell, and Jackson can too, because as we're being walked to our table, which is in the middle of the restaurant and could seat about twelve, the man, who must be the manager, is apologizing.

"Of course I understand," Jackson says, cutting him off. "But it is helpful to have staff that can prepare for these types of things, isn't it? I know several people spoke to you—"

"Yes, and I'm sorry for any problems," the manager says. "I'll be sure to bring you your food myself."

"Excellent," Jackson says. "I want something special for Hannah. The best in the house." He touches my arm, and the manager smiles at me, a wide, shiny smile that doesn't reach his eyes.

"Of course."

He disappears, the offending hostess in tow, and I see her being sent into the back. A girl working behind the long, polished counter that's packed with people ordering chocolate coffee drinks is beckoned, and she moves smoothly forward, bends in close to the manager as he talks, and then nods.

She's at our table about five seconds later, smiling at Jackson and telling him that she's a huge fan of his show and is "So Thrilled!" to meet him.

"Would you sign this for me?" she says, picking up a napkin from the empty seat next to mine and handing it to him.

"I'd love to," Jackson says. "What's your name, sweetheart?"

"Megan."

"You know, I'm going to dinner at nine tonight and I'd love it if you could join us," Jackson says, sliding a card out of his shirt pocket. "Just call this number and Fran, my assistant, will get you the details."

"I'll definitely try to be there," Megan says. "In the meantime, if you need anything, let me know." She winks at him before she walks away.

"Lovely," Jackson says. "Reminds me of a girl I met back in 1985. She ended up having a daughter who posed for us just last year. Do you think that man who just waved at me would like an autograph?"

"I . . ." I say, and glance over at the man, who doesn't appear to be doing anything except demolishing a huge sundae and staring at the new hostess's body as she ushers people to their seats. He's not even looking in our direction. "I think he's probably respecting your privacy."

"New Yorkers are great about that," he says. "Although in the past, I used to get mobbed everywhere."

He sounds sad—not a lot, but I hear it—and I realize he knows he's not the star he once was. I thought Jackson never saw things he didn't want to. But he sees this, and he saw that

Mom needed me all those years ago. Still needs me.

Maybe I've been a little too hard on him. I lean into him then, a sort of hug. It feels strange, but familiar too, and he puts one arm around me and whispers, "Thank you, Princess."

I'm glad I came. I'm glad I took a chance with Jackson. With my dad.

I smile at him, and he smiles back.

I think someone—probably the new hostess—will come by and give us menus, but instead food just shows up. It's delivered by the chef who owns and runs the restaurant, a short, ginger-haired man who shakes Jackson's hand enthusiastically, raves about some girl he saw a picture of on the site about a decade ago, and then says, "Should I repeat that when the cameras arrive?"

"No cameras today, I'm afraid," Jackson says, and the chef stiffens and glares at the manager, who goes pale as the chef abruptly heads back into the kitchen.

"Mr. James, I was told that—" the manager says, and Jackson says, "Is this whole milk you've given me? Because it doesn't taste like it."

"It is," the manager says stiffly.

"Are you sure?"

"Yes, sir, I am."

Jackson shakes his head and puts the glass down, then turns to me, dismissing the manager, who doesn't leave until Darryl leans over and whispers something to him that makes the manager go even paler before he dashes off into the kitchen.

"And what did you get?" Jackson says.

"I don't know." I actually wanted the chocolate cake I saw

when we came in, but what I've got is some sort of tower of brittle chocolate pieces that I can't figure out how to eat. A fork shatters them, and I don't see anyone else eating with their hands.

"Well, it looks wonderful," Jackson says. "And seeing you sitting here, knowing you're here . . . it's magical, it really is." He smiles at me. "You know what? You should spend the night. I'll get you a room at the hotel and Fran can arrange for you to go back in the morning instead of tonight. What do you say?"

"I thought you were going out tonight."

"I'll send the girls out and stay in with you," he says. "We'll send someone to get my favorite movies and then we'll relax, have some popcorn, and keep catching up. I'll call Fran and have her take care of everything, all right, Princess?"

"Well—"

"Jackson!" a voice shrieks, and I turn and see a dark-haired girl coming through the door, skirt hiked up high on her tan thighs, shirt cut low on her generous chest. There are four more almost identical-looking girls behind her. There's also a camera crew, which is zooming in on Jackson.

And then me.

twenty-three

"Brandi, darling, what are you doing here?" Jackson says, sounding surprised, and Brandi looks confused and says, "You said we had to be here by—"

"Brandi, what are you going to get?" Sandi—another "special girl"—says, sitting down on Jackson's other side and shooting her a quick, hard look.

"I'm going to get EVERYTHING," Brandi says, and grins at the camera.

Sandi is the only one of Jackson's girls I recognize from before, and she looks exactly the same and yet somehow harder, like she's been shellacked into her "look."

"It's such an amazing surprise to see you," she says. "And you look fantastic!"

I can almost feel the camera zooming in on me, and I look at Jackson. "Can I talk to you?"

"I thought that's what we were doing," he says, and grins at the girls and the camera. I don't know any of them other than Sandi, but they all have the Jackson "special girl" look: long dark hair, tiny body, and huge chest. One of them can't be more than a year older than me, although it's hard to tell with all the makeup she's wearing. Sandi, who must be about twenty-three now, has so much on that she looks like she's wearing a mask.

"Terri, Alli, and Mindi," Jackson says, looking at three of the girls I've never seen before, "this is my daughter, Hannah. Brandi and Sandi, I think you've met her before."

"Nope, I've just been here for a year, remember, honey?" Brandi says with what looks like a slight eye roll at the cameras, and then glances at me. "You should totally wear your hair down. You'd be hot if you did. Want me to help you with it later before we go out?"

He lied to me. He lied to me and I actually fell for it. I told myself I wouldn't get sucked in, but I did.

I'm so stupid.

I put my fork down. I stand up. I nod when Sandi says, "Are you all right?" and the camera zooms in on her, then me.

"Just need to use the bathroom," I say, and Brandi and one of the other girls say, "Oh, me too!" and before I know it, I'm swept into the bathroom in a cloud of perfume and chatter.

"Oh my God, my boobs hurt like you wouldn't believe," the girl who doesn't look much older than me says as soon as we walk in. She lifts up her shirt and starts rubbing the sides of her breasts.

She turns to me. "Sorry, but I'm, like, dying. I got the biggest implants, and I don't know if I have enough skin to cover them. But I figure, when else am I going to turn nineteen? And who else would get me a gift like this? Your dad is so amazing, by the way. Living with him is a total dream come true."

"The cameras aren't in here, idiot," Brandi says, and looks at me. "You didn't know we were coming, right? I tried to give you a heads-up when I came in because I saw what happened the last time you were on the show. I was, like, fifteen and it was all me and my friends talked about for a week."

"He planned this," I say, and my voice comes out thick and choked-sounding.

"Well, sort of. The TV people wanted it to happen, so . . ." Brandi trails off. "But he does talk about you. And it'll be fun to hang out and I really will fix your hair and stuff, because you could be hot if you wanted to. Just don't tell Sandi I told you anything about the cameras being planned, okay? She blabs to Jackson about everything, and he's already mad at me for telling Darryl he looked hot the other day."

"I won't tell," I say, and walk out of the bathroom.

I don't go back into the restaurant. I walk into the kitchen, which is loud and crowded. At least three people tell me to get out—yell, actually—but I ignore them. There has to be a way out of here.

Someone grabs my arm.

It's the chef, the red-haired guy who came out to see us before. "Tell me the fucking cameras showed," he says. "I was promised on-air publicity for giving up that table for two hours."

143

"The cameras showed," I say, and he practically knocks me over on his way out into the restaurant.

The hostess who Jackson sent away before is standing over to one side of the kitchen, looking upset, and when she sees me, she waves me over.

"Hey, is that guy your dad?" she says.

"Yeah." I'm too upset to lie.

"He's so old. I mean, he looks okay, but he's just—"

"He is old," I say. "He's ancient. And I'm sorry about before. He doesn't think about what he does, or how it affects other people. You didn't get fired, did you?"

She shakes her head. "We get people like him in here all the time and it's like, hi, this is New York, there are people so much more famous than you around."

I nod. "Is there a back door or something around here?"

"Looking for a way out?"

"Yeah."

She smiles. "Come with me."

She takes me to a door that leads into a narrow hallway.

"It'll take you out to the street," she says. "You'll come out farther down, away from the restaurant."

"Thanks," I tell her, and then head down the hallway. I'm not exactly sure where I am, but I know Penn Station is near 34th Street and I'm sure I can walk there from here. Manhattan isn't that big, after all, and I've seen the map of the subway that Teagan has up on the wall in her bedroom.

Not that I can remember anything about the subway. Or have money to pay for it. But still, at least I know where I'm going.

144

The hallway is pretty long, and I figure I'll end up far away from the restaurant. Maybe I won't even have that far to walk to get to Penn Station.

I reach the end, open the door, and walk outside.

"There you are," Jackson says, and I stare at him, stunned. "I was so worried when you didn't come back." He turns to someone standing next to him—the girl I just talked to, the hostess he was mean to before. "Thank you so much for telling me she got turned around."

"Sure," she says. "I knew you'd want to know. And, well, I know this is sort of bold, but I would love to send you my picture. I think I'd be perfect for your site. In fact, if you want, you can see my modeling portfolio at thaliatart.com."

And the camera, the ever-present stupid camera, zooms in on her as she smiles. Getting her three seconds of fame.

I don't know why I ever listen to anyone.

The camera swings back to me, and I stand there, looking at it, as Jackson says, "Hannah, are you all right? I know you haven't been to the city since your stepfather died, but don't worry, I'm looking out for you."

That bastard. Still pretending to care.

Always pretending.

I take a deep breath, and hear the camera whir as it zooms in on me, waiting.

They can wait till the world ends because I won't give them or Jackson the satisfaction of what they all want. I won't give them anything they can use for the stupid show.

I step around Jackson like he's nothing—and he is, he is—

and out into the street. It's later than I thought, the sun just starting to set, and yet it's still crowded, the sidewalk packed with fast-moving people.

I feel slow, stupid, and force myself to walk, to pretend I don't notice people looking annoyed as they move around me.

"Hannah?" It's Jackson. He's calling me, but I know that's all he'll do. He won't come after me. He's too old to run.

And I'm not worth it. Not to him.

"Hannah," someone else says, grabbing my arm, and I turn to see Darryl, with Sandi by his side. She looks a bit winded and wobbly.

"Too many drinks at lunch," she says, and winks at the camera that's following along behind her. "Hannah, sweetie, your father wants to know what's going on. Are you mad at him or something?"

"I have to go," I say. "He knows that. He only brought me here for the day. He must have forgotten to tell you." I will not say anything else. "Maybe you should have his doctor check to make sure he's not going senile or something."

Well, I figure saying one thing is okay.

"You are angry at him. But why?" Sandi says, wide-eyed, and I force myself to smile at her as I step away from Darryl.

"I'm not angry. I just need to get to the train station."

"But we had plans to go out and—"

"Really? Jackson never said anything about going out to me. You can even ask Darryl—I mean, he was with us the whole time."

Sandi's smile stays, but her eyes scream quit-being-a-pain-in-the-ass at me. "That's so weird, because we got you a dress and everything. And . . . well, promise you won't tell Jackson I told you, but he's planned a special dinner for you too. You do—you do want to be here, right? You do want to see your father?"

Oh, now I can see why she's lasted so long with Jackson. She's as good an actor as he is.

"Well, see, my train ticket clearly says I'm leaving today," I say, and pull it out, pressing it against the camera when it doesn't move in closer. "In just a little while, even. Strange how last minute the whole party thing seems, huh? Almost like . . . I don't know. A ratings stunt, or something. Anyway, I should get going."

And then I turn around and walk. I walk as fast as I can, and soon Sandi's gone, winded or fallen over or run off to tell Jackson. Don't know. Don't care. The camera is still there, though, and the woman holding it says, in a sympathetic voice, "He didn't tell you we were coming to meet you, did he?"

I pretend I can't hear her and keep walking. The street signs say I'm barely in the 20s, and I don't know which way to go when I get to 34th Street. It doesn't matter, though. I'm not going back.

"Wait, hold up," another female voice yells, and Brandi catches up to me, breathing hard and holding her side. "I fucking hate running in heels. It should totally be a professional sport," she laughs, turning to the camera.

And then, still smiling, she says, "Turn that damn thing off or I'll tell Jackson about the night you came on to me."

The camerawoman stiffens, looks pissed, and then drops back.

"Camera down and actually turned off," Brandi says, and

stills me, holding my arm as she watches the camera and the woman holding it.

"Everyone thinks I'm dumb," Brandi says once the camera's off and we've walked a few feet away. "It's so annoying. I swear, when my two years with the show are up, I'm out of here. Pretending that Jackson's hot and that his stories don't suck—I'm not that good an actress. Not yet, anyway."

She turns to me. "And you know, he never asks how I am, or anything like that, and I live with him. It's like he really believes it's okay for him to not even pretend to give a shit. Anyway, good for you for leaving."

"I—"

"No time," she says, shaking her head, and presses something into my hand. "I have to get back, but if you walk two streets over to the left, hold up your arm, and—wait . . ." She reaches over and pulls the elastic around my ponytail free, so my hair falls down around me. "There. Now you'll be able to get a cab."

And then she turns around and runs back to the camera, smiling at passersby as the woman picks it up and turns it on again.

I walk, keeping pace with the people around me, and Brandi was right. Two blocks over, and with my hair down, I'm able to get a cab. And with the twenty she's slipped me, I'm able to pay for a ride to Penn Station.

I wait for my train in silent misery, alone in an ever-changing crowd. Jackson doesn't come looking for me.

I don't let myself cry until I'm on the train, and even then I do it in the bathroom, where I'm sure no one will see me. I cry and look at myself in the warped, small mirror, and hate myself for being so stupid. For thinking Jackson could ever be sincere.

For thinking, if only for a little while, that he really wanted to see me, and for how much it hurts that he didn't.

twenty-four

Mom's waiting for me when I get off the train, and even though I'd splashed tepid, metallic-smelling water on my face in the bathroom—immediately regretting it because all I smelled was that water for the rest of the way home—she can tell I've been crying.

"What happened?" is the first thing she says, and when I don't reply, she says, "Oh, Hannah," and puts an arm around me.

I hug her, for once not caring that she's in a skirt the size of a handkerchief and a shirt that's just a little bit larger. I'm just glad to know that I'm with someone who cares about me for real.

"Mom, about this morning—"

"Shhhh," she says. "We don't have to talk about that now. Fran called me a while ago, probably right before you left. She

told me you'd gotten upset about the cameras, and that Jackson
was sorry you wouldn't stay longer. I could tell she was being
taped. I guess he . . ."

"Yeah," I say. "Lied."

"I'm sorry," Mom says, and on the way home, she stops at
Taco Town and buys a big thing of nachos, the kind that come
with cheese and sour cream and beef and tons of other stuff, all
looking like it was shot out of some industrial food gun.

"You must be hungry," she says, and hands me the bag. I
open it and then set it on the seat between us. I like nachos fine,
but Mom likes them more. After José died, she ate them every day,
twice a day, for two weeks, until she couldn't fit into the sweat-
pants she'd been wearing.

"I'm sorry Jackson lied to you like he did," she says as we
pull back onto the road. "I thought . . . it's been so long since he's
seen you that I'd hoped—"

"But you thought he might do what he did."

She eats one chip, then two, then a handful, too many to fit
in her mouth and there's something almost manic about how she's
chewing so fast, like she's trying to fill something inside her.

Or not talk.

"Mom?" I say, and she sighs, dropping the chips she's picked
up back into the bag.

"I think he believes what he says when he says it," she
says. "That's one of the things that make Jackson so difficult to
really know. He just . . . his world is so different from anyone
else's. It's—"

"All about him," I say, the words bitter in my mouth. "He just assumed I'd be so glad to be with him that I'd see the cameras and everything else he did as—I don't know."

"He thinks that because he wants something, you'll want it too," Mom says. "But, Hannah, he's not—"

"Don't," I say, picking at the chips, too angry to eat—which is not something that usually happens to me. "Please don't say he's not a bad guy."

"That's not what I was going to say."

"Oh."

"He's charming, and when you're with him, you feel . . . I always felt like Jackson needed me. Like I was important to him, and not just because of the sex."

Eww. "Mom."

"I really thought he liked being with me," she says. "And you wouldn't be here if he and I hadn't—"

"I know. But I still don't want to hear about it."

She sighs. "Anyway, the problem is that while Jackson does care, he isn't able to—"

"Tell the truth?"

"It's more like he can't handle being around people who are upset. He just—it bothers him, and so he thinks that if he goes ahead with what he wants, it'll all work out. And it usually does, because he's a giving man and a sweet one—"

I snort, but it comes out more like a sob, and I think of Jackson, smiling at me and saying today was all about me. How it seemed like he really meant it.

"Why did you let me go see him? You must have known what would happen."

"I hoped it wouldn't. I just . . . I thought it might work out. I mean, he called you. That's a big deal."

I crumple a few chips in my fingers, not looking at her, but she must know what I'm thinking because she says, "I guess you thought so too," her voice sad.

"Yeah. I mean, he did call, and he . . . he was so nice to me when I got there. He said he wanted to spend the day with me. Said it would just be me and him. He even asked me to spend the night. Of course, then the cameras showed up."

"He asked you to stay? To not come home? Did you—did you want to do that?" Her voice rises a little on the last words, and I look over at her. There's a tiny smear of cheese on her chin, and Jackson was right about one thing.

Not that Mom can't live without me, but that she loves me. Loves me enough that if Jackson had said yes all those years ago, she would have let me move in with him. It would have hurt her, but she loves me enough to think about me before she thinks about herself.

She loves me for real, and not for cameras and ratings.

She loves me enough to be my mom.

"I didn't want to stay," I say. "And now I just want to go home and forget Jackson exists."

"He might call and say he's . . ." Mom trails off.

"Yeah, we both know he won't apologize," I say. "I'm sure he'll call again, but not until the next time he wants something."

"He does care about you, Hannah," Mom says. "I really believe that. He just—"

"Cares about himself more," I say, and she reaches over and squeezes my hand.

"Are you mad at me?"

"No," I say, because I'm not. I'm not even mad at Jackson now. (All right, I am, but it's more of an exhausted angry, the kind of anger that makes you tired and sad, and I know, from past experience, that thinking about it goes nowhere.)

Once we're home, I spend the weekend in bed. I can't face anything or anyone right now, so I call in sick to work and skip my Saturday shift to imagine elaborate scenarios in which the New York trip goes very different, most ending with me telling Jackson . . .

Nothing. I've got nothing. How can you hurt someone who doesn't care enough about anyone—about you—to be hurt?

Teagan calls once, on Saturday night, but I have Mom tell her I'm sick, and she brings me some macaroni and cheese after that. "How long are you planning on being in here?"

"A while."

She sits down next to me on my bed and plucks a piece of macaroni and cheese out of the pot. "I wish I had something smart to say."

"You're here, and you made me something to eat." But I secretly wish she had something smart to say too. Something that would make me stop replaying those moments in New York when I was happy, when I believed Jackson wanted to see me.

When I was so stupid.

twenty-five

By Sunday afternoon, I'm not ready to leave the
house, but I'm more than ready for a shower. Afterward, I take the
twenty I keep for emergencies out of my top dresser drawer and
order a pizza.

Mom comes out of the den when it arrives, dressed in an
extremely abbreviated nurse's outfit, which has been unbuttoned
enough to show off a bright red bra.

"Don't tell me," I say when she sees me looking, and open
the pizza box.

"Can I have half a slice?" she says.

"Sure," I say, and go get a knife so she can cut a piece in half.
I pick up the cheese she pulls off and put it on my own slice.

"I wish I could still eat like that," she says.

"You could."

"Not if I wanted people to pay money for—" She gestures at herself. "Hey, does this mean you're actually up now?"

"I guess."

"Good," she says, and leans over and kisses my cheek. "You'll let me pay you back for this?"

I shake my head. "It's just a pizza. Save your money, and let's have light for another month."

She laughs. "It's not that bad. Not this month, anyway. Okay, back to work."

"Thanks for taking a break and eating—well, part of a piece of pizza."

She smiles at me, then comes over, bends down, and kisses the top of my head. It's nice, but it reminds me of Jackson, stupid lying Jackson.

It also reminds me that I don't need to see so much of my mother's cleavage.

"Moooom," I say, and she pulls back and laughs.

I make a face at her but don't really mean it, and she can tell because she's humming as she goes back to work. I eat another slice of pizza, then put the rest in the fridge and go do some homework. I figure I'll work till around ten, and then call Teagan and tell her about the disaster that was Friday.

So I have my evening all planned out, and I work on my homework and eat another slice of pizza. No one calls, but that's okay. It's not like I expected Jackson to call. I know he's not going to apologize or anything like that, and I really didn't think he'd care if I got home okay or not.

Except I did. Just a little, but still, I did. I mean, I'm his daughter, and him not calling reminds me there's a reason I call him Jackson and not Dad. That there's a reason I didn't talk to him for five years.

But it's done now. That chapter of my life is over.

Or so I think until 10:03, which is when Mom comes up to my room and says, "Hannah, there's something you'd better see."

"What?"

"Just come with me," she says, sounding very unhappy, and I follow her downstairs and into the den.

Mom sits down at her computer, and a moment later a promo for Jackson's show appears. The network puts up a new clip every week, highlighting an upcoming episode.

The minute I see the words "Jackson James: Family," I know what I'm going to see.

I know and yet I watch as Jackson "chats" with his "special girls," who are all dressed in lingerie or covered by network-placed black bars, and talks about how much he misses his dear, dead parents. And how much he loves his dear, sweet daughter.

Cut to a shot of me screaming at him when I was twelve.

"It's been too long since I've seen her," Jackson says to the camera, his eyes welling with tears.

Cut to audio of me from Friday saying I'm leaving as an image of Jackson's hurt face is frozen on-screen.

Cut to Jackson smiling at Sandi as she pretends to frolic in clothes that are too short and tight to allow any real movement.

"I feel like I have it all," he says. "But sometimes I wish . . ." He sighs.

Cut to Jackson hanging up the phone and saying, "She's coming to see me! Hannah's coming. It's a dream come true."

And then there we are in the restaurant. Is there a shot of the shock on my face when the girls show up?

Of course not. Just me saying I'm going to the bathroom, the camera zooming in on my upset-looking face, and then that horrible, lying hostess saying, "If Jackson James was my dad, I'd be a lot less bitchy to him. I mean, he's a legend, you know?"

Cut to Jackson looking concerned, and Sandi saying, "It'll be all right, we'll find her, honey," as one of the other girls says, "Oh my God, she just left without saying anything?"

I notice Brandi isn't in any of the shots.

Then there's me, walking out of the restaurant's back exit and seeing Jackson. Me walking away. Jackson looking surprised and hurt.

The promo closes with Sandi saying, "He loves her so much. I don't understand how Hannah can be so cruel," and one last shot of me staring, with pure hate, at the camera. Like I'm looking at Jackson, only I wasn't. I was looking at the awful camerawoman Brandi got rid of.

But it doesn't matter. This is Jackson's truth, and it'll go to a hell of a lot more people than mine will.

The promo disappears, and Mom is holding my hand. "Hannah?"

"I'm fine," I say, and force myself to smile at her. "I knew as soon as I saw the cameras that everything would end up . . . well, like this."

"There's more."

"More?"

Mom fiddles with the collar of her nurse's outfit. "I— Teagan's here, in the kitchen. She just got off work. Apparently she was working late tonight because her store was having a special Sunday night sale and a lot of her customers were . . . I guess they must go to school with you. And they've seen what you just did."

"Teagan's here?" She knows how I feel about people coming over, and things must be really, really bad if she's done it. And told Mom what was going on.

But how would anyone even know about my trip? I didn't decide to go until the last minute. The only time it ever came up anywhere was at work and . . .

Work. Where both Finn and Josh heard me talking to Jackson. And where I mentioned a trip.

Finn. He knew I was going to New York.

No, Finn wouldn't do that sort of thing. He can be a pain sometimes, but overall he's . . . well, nice. Sweet, even.

But if he'd mentioned the phone call I'd gotten at work, even for a second, to Brent, or any of Brent's troglodyte friends . . .

Yeah, that would do it.

Except I can't even see Finn doing that, if only because he never told anyone about the time two months ago when Mom showed up at work, frantic because she'd forgotten to pay our electricity bill and we were going to lose power if she didn't take them $290 by 6 P.M.

Finn's never mentioned her visit, or how I had to leave work with her for a little while so I could get money out of my bank account from the nearest ATM. In fact, the only thing he did was give me sandwiches from the sub place down the street every night that week because the girl working behind the counter knew his older sister and kept giving him free food.

And Josh would never say anything. He's just not that kind of guy. He's better than a regular guy. He was beyond nice when Mom came in too, and even offered to walk her to her car when we got back from the ATM because it gets sort of dark in the parking lot. Mom refused, but called him "sweet" and blew him a kiss before she left. I apologized afterward, and Josh was very nice about it. He even asked how Mom was the next day.

"I'd better go talk to Teagan," I say to Mom now.

Mom opens her mouth, like she's going to say something else, but then just squeezes my hand and says, "Come get me if you need anything, okay?"

Which just goes to show how bad things are. Mom has never told me to come get her if I need something while she's working. Ever.

I definitely have to talk to Teagan, and head for the kitchen.

"You saw it?" she says when I come in. She's sitting at the kitchen table, looking upset.

"Just now. I guess you did too?"

"Yeah," she says. "Well, bits and pieces. I heard all of it, though. There were a bunch of people from Slaterville High in at eight, never mind that we were closing at eight-thirty, and they kept unfolding jeans and not trying them on until I wanted to strangle them, or, better yet, make them fold all the jeans and—"

"Teagan."

"Sorry. They were talking about the promo, and watching it on their phones. I guess somebody saw it when it first got posted and told someone, and they told someone else, and . . . well, you know."

"Who was there?"

"A bunch of girls and a couple of guys, including this one moron who called me a lesbian when I said I didn't want his phone number."

"Let me guess," I said, dread bubbling in my stomach. "His name was Brent."

She nods. "Is that the Brent you've told me about? He really is an ass."

"Yeah," I say, sitting down next to Teagan. "I can't wait for school tomorrow."

"Sorry. And I'm sorry I just came over like this, but I knew you'd want to know. This is—"

"Yeah. It's sucktastic," I say, resting my head on the table. "I would ask how people found out, but I already know. What I've got to figure out is, who told Brent?"

"Maybe no one did," Teagan says, and I look at her. "I mean, obviously, someone did, but I don't think he knew first. One of the girls there . . . well, she seemed to really not like you. Or your mother. She did most of the talking about you, actually."

A girl? "What did she look like?"

"Pretty. Dark hair. Which I know doesn't narrow it down, but she didn't buy anything so I don't have a name or anything like that."

"And you think she's the one who found the clip?"

Teagan shrugs. "I don't know. I just know she isn't a fan of yours. And that she really, really doesn't like your mother."

"But how would she know I went to New York?"

"I don't know," Teagan says again. "I'm sorry."

I get up and grab the pizza from the fridge. "You want something to eat?"

"Hell, yes. I mean, yes, please."

I grin at her and pass her the box. "I'm sorry about not talking to you on Saturday, but I just—"

"Needed to hide out?"

"Exactly."

"Pretty soon you can come do it at my place, if you want."

"Your place?"

"I got an apartment. One bedroom, a kitchen, and a living room. All for about a quarter of what I paid for my tiny closet room in New York. I'm moving in next week."

"What about school?"

"I'm not going back," she says. "I told my parents I'm just not ready. I figure I'll tell them about the flunking out part later. A lot later."

"But you could go to another school and—"

"I'm not going back," she says again.

"What if I come over tomorrow and help you fill out applications?"

"You're not going to school?"

"Would you?"

"Well, no, but since when do you care what anyone in Slaterville thinks about you?"

"I don't care, I just don't feel like dealing with any crap," I say, but the thing is, I do care. And I know what people say about not listening to insults or how you should let stuff roll off you, but it's not that easy.

I'm not saying words are big jagged rocks or anything, but I'm already flayed raw by Jackson. Mockery for being turned into a monster by my so-called father isn't going to help.

"You should go," she says. "Go and when they say shit, picture them where I am. You think Brent's going to become a football star? He'll go to a fourth-rate college, never play a game, and then get engaged to some girl from around here who remembers when he was a big deal. Twenty years from now, you'll come back totally successful and—"

"I'll look perfect and he'll have to pump my gas and then he'll confess he's always been in love with me—come on, Teagan. He's going to go to college and graduate and get a job and become the kind of guy who gets promoted because he sucks up to the boss and backstabs everyone else. But thanks for trying."

"Okay then, here's why you have to go," she says. "You don't show up, and they'll know why. Sharks smell blood, and I spent all of high school bleeding into the water for making my own clothes and for—"

"Being your own person."

"That's a really nice way to say 'weird,'" she says. "But I was weird, Hannah, and you—"

"I know. With my mom and Jackson, I'm weird too."

"Yeah," she says. "But the fact that you try so hard to be unnoticeable makes you stand out even more."

"I don't try to be unnoticeable. I just—"

"Please, this is me," Teagan says. "Besides, how many girls wear their hair scraped back from their face with no makeup and clothes that look like they belong to a lost giant?"

"It's a ponytail, and I like comfortable clothes."

She laughs. "Okay, fine, I take it back. Your clothes look like they belong to a lost almost giant. Better?"

I stick my tongue out at her.

"It won't be that bad if you go," she says.

"Liar."

"Well, okay, it'll suck. But you can talk to Josh about it. He was nice to you the other day, right?"

"So tomorrow I should see if he'll talk to me out of pity, and hope that pity translates into him asking me out?"

"What, you can't do that?"

"No, sadly, I can," I say. "Pity's all I've got going for me. I guess I might as well use it."

"You've got more than pity going—oh, forget it," Teagan says. "You're so terrible at taking compliments I'm not even going to try."

"Thank you," I say. "And hey, doesn't that prove I can take a compliment?"

"No, you freak," she says, getting up. "See you tomorrow after work?"

"Yeah," I say, and decide that I am going to get over myself and my worries and will finally really and truly talk to Josh. I've got nothing left to lose, after all, and maybe, in the end, tomorrow won't be that bad.

twenty-six

But, of course, it is that bad.

As soon as I get to school I get *the look* from what seems like everyone. I haven't seen *the look* since I first moved here but it's still the same, a smile that's all smirk followed by staring or laughter. Or both. I'm used to blending in—and I like it—so *the look* is a very, very unwelcome visitor. But not a surprise.

Thanks, Jackson.

"Hey," Nikki White says, and I freeze. Nikki is one of those brittle, beautiful girls who are like flowers crossed with something thorny and poisonous, the ones everyone says they like but are mostly terrified of. She's definitely got *the look* going, and normally I avoid this sort of thing by pretending I don't hear or see anything. I can't do that today, though, so I stop and face her because if I don't things will get worse. I learned that in middle school, yet another lesson that proved people are wrong about so many things. Ignoring something doesn't make it go away when it comes to stuff like this—it just makes people yell louder or meaner until you listen and take your humiliation.

"I got sent this video this morning," Nikki says, holding out her phone so I can see a grainy picture of my angry face. "It's you, right? I'd kill myself if that creepy old guy was my dad. And you went and saw him? Eww. Do you want to be one of those girls on his pathetic site or something?"

I stay silent—believe me, talking will not help here—and she finally wears herself out going over what she's just said in different ways and sways off. I wish I knew she was the one Teagan saw last night, the one who supposedly hates me and really hates Mom, but I know she isn't. She has no idea who I am, not really. She's just someone who's noticed me because of the video and she'll forget what she's said before the day is over.

Me? Not so much, but I go on, my legs shaking and a mix of anger and despair burning inside me.

I pass Brent on the way to my locker, but all he's got to say is that Jackson is a "weird old guy" with "hot babes who clearly wish they were with real men." That's nothing after what I've just heard, and when he goes off on a tangent about what he'd like to do with Jackson's "special girls," I slip away.

All this, and it's not even first period.

I go to my classes and either stare at my desk or the board the whole time. And when I see people I know—meaning Michelle—

I make sure she doesn't have to deal with me. I wait until after the bell has rung for gym before I go, and when I finally get there, the only open seat left is up front and far away from her. I think she looks grateful when I sit down, but then she comes up to me in the hall after class.

"I saw the video," she says, and I look at her, surprised and kind of—well, kind of hurt. I mean, I don't think Michelle will say anything as bad as the whole "go kill yourself" thing, but I thought she liked me at least a little.

"Your . . . um, dad seems . . . different," she says. "I mean, all he talked about was how he felt, and he didn't really seem to— I don't know. Think about stuff. I actually thought he seemed like an . . ." She pauses, and then whispers, "Ass."

That is so not what I expected to hear. "Really?"

"Yeah, but I don't know him, so I guess—"

"No, you're right," I say. "He's an ass."

"Sorry. That really sucks," she says, and heads off to her next class.

Wow. Someone said something nice to me. At school. Today.

I'm able to get through lunch on that, although eating a so-called hamburger while I sit near the freshman outcasts isn't a whole lot of fun.

I do overhear them saying that someone punched Brent, though, and that is fun.

In Government, Finn shoots me a concerned look as he sits down, and I return it with a bland one of my own, pretending I'm totally fine.

The thing is, even pretending is hard right now, so I quickly look away.

He tosses me a note about ten minutes into class.

"You okay?"

I look at him and don't bother to write back.

Another note lands on my desk about a minute later.

"Sorry about everything. I heard Brent say some girl told him about the Jackson thing yesterday."

Who is this girl? I write back. "Do you know who she is?"

"No," he writes back, and then raises his hand and says he has to go talk to Mr. Landon, one of the football coaches.

"All right," our teacher says, "but please remind Mr. Landon he should talk to me beforehand about this sort of thing, especially since football season is over." She's trying to sound tough, but she's blushing because—as everyone knows—she has a crush on Mr. Landon. (I guess the dating pool is real small when you're a teacher.)

"Thanks," Finn says. "The thing is, I have this—" He leans over and picks up an obviously heavy bag. "I've got to take it to him, and I've got another one in my locker, so I was thinking someone should come with me."

"Nice try, Finn," our teacher says, sighing. "However, I'm not letting you and one of your friends leave together."

"Fine, I'll go with—I don't know," Finn says, and then points at me. "Hannah, I guess. Can she come?"

The teacher nods, and I glare at him but have to get up now because everyone's looking at us. At me. On our way out, one of his teammates says, "Dude, ask her about that video," and Finn stumbles and cracks his book against the guy's knee.

"Shit, that hurts," the guy says, and the teacher says, "Language!" as she shoos us out into the hall.

When we're there, Finn tosses the heavy bag at me. I move out of the way automatically, but it still lands on my foot.

"Ow," I say, and then realize my foot doesn't hurt. In fact, the bag feels empty.

"What's in here?" I ask him.

"Nothing now," he says, scooping it up and heading down the hall. "Before it had a bunch of flyers for a bake sale the team parents are having next weekend, but I stuck them in my locker so I wouldn't have to lug them around."

"So why did you do all that in class just now?"

"To leave, obviously." He turns back and looks at me. "Come on."

I follow, a little cautiously, but catch up quickly when Finn stops at the vending machines. He buys two bags of chips, a granola bar, an orange juice, and a bag of animal crackers.

"Here," he says, and hands me a bag of chips, the granola bar, and the orange juice.

"Oh," I say. "Thanks, but I really can't take—"

"Yeah, you can. I saw you in the cafeteria with one of those so-called burgers. You won't even make it through an hour at work on that. And I'm not taking all your orders."

"You saw me at lunch?"

"Yep, we share something besides Government," he says. "I gotta get those flyers out of my locker and into my car so Coach

Landon won't explode. Eat, okay? You're useless to me otherwise."

I sort of want to hug him. A lot. It's strange—but nice—and I smile at him. "How come I don't get the animal crackers?"

"Greedy," he says, grinning, and hands them over. "You sure you're okay?"

I nod, and he looks at my mouth, then blushes and says, "See you later."

I can't say anything because I'm too busy being stunned that Finn looked at my mouth. And that I definitely noticed him looking.

twenty-seven

Because Slaterville High is so big, they don't let everyone out at once when school ends. If they did, it would screw up traffic for ages, and as it is now, I'm on last bell and still spend about ten minutes waiting to get out of the parking lot.

Normally, I don't mind sitting around last period waiting to leave, but today I'm more than ready to get out of here. I twist around in my seat and look at the clock. Two more minutes. I turn back around, but not before I see another version of *the look*. I wish I'd just left school after Finn got me out of Government. I don't know why I didn't, now. I guess I was too busy thinking about stuff.

Like how nice Finn has been today. How he's actually usually not that bad, even.

And how he looked at me.

I look at the clock again. One more minute. Still getting *the look*. Ugh.

Finally, the last bell rings, and I head out to the parking lot, wondering if I have time to go home and hide under my comforter for a while before I go to work, and if that makes me pathetic, or weird, or both.

"Hannah?"

"Josh?" I say, turning around.

It is him, and he looks amazing, like always. I try not to stare too much, but it's hard.

"Hey, what are you doing now?" he says.

"Going to work. Well, I'm going home first, for just a little while, and then I'm going to work." Oh good, I'm finally talking—only I'm saying the most boring things ever. Why does this happen around him? Why?

"I'm supposed to work today too," he says. "But I think I'm going to call in sick."

"Oh. I didn't know—you don't look—I mean, I'm sorry you're sick." He hasn't mentioned Jackson or the stupid video or anything like that, but then, I knew he wouldn't. Too bad my pity plan isn't working very well. Unless he decides to take pity on me for not being able to speak in complete sentences.

"Well, the thing is," he says, taking a step closer, and he's so gorgeous he's almost unreal-looking, with those dark eyes and dark hair. Not to mention that he's tall and lean and even has gorgeous elbows, his skin all smooth and golden.

Wait, has he stopped talking? Crap, he has, and I've totally missed what he said! What do I do now? Smile and nod? Smile?

Look concerned? I can't say, "Sorry, I was so busy looking at you I didn't hear you."

"Okay," he says, blowing out a breath and looking so adorably nervous that I swear, it's like he's practiced it or something. "I guess that's a no, then?"

"It's not that, it's just—" Please jump in and repeat what you said. Please.

"You know Greg won't even notice if you call in sick," Josh says. "He never listens to his messages anyway. And Finn knows how to route extra orders over to another call room. I just . . . I thought it would be nice if we could hang out, that's all."

He's asked me out.

Josh has asked me out!

"I'll call Greg," I say. "I have to do it at home because I don't have a cell, but then maybe we could . . ." What am I supposed to say now? I know nothing about hanging out with guys.

"Great," Josh says. "I'll come over to your house around four, okay?"

I nod, and he grins at me and starts to walk away.

Josh! Me! Josh and me! It's really happening, finally. Josh is coming over. He's coming to my house. He's going to be in my house.

Oh no, he's going to be in my house. With me.

And Mom.

"Wait," I say, panicked, and he turns around.

"You don't have to come over. We could meet somewhere instead. I mean, I haven't even given you directions or—"

"I know where you live," he says, and winks at me. "See you soon."

He knows where I live?

He knows where I live!

I race home, dreaming of Josh sitting next to me on the sofa, putting his arm around me as we watch a movie (do Mom and I still have cable?) and then he'll pull me close and—

And then Mom will wander by in her underwear.

Okay, I can fix this.

I think.

I find Mom lying on the living room floor doing leg lifts and crunches. She's wearing a sports bra and shorts, which is more than usual, but still. Not enough.

"Hey," she says. "What are you doing home before work?"

"I'm not going to work. And you have to get dressed. As in real clothes, Mom."

"What? And why aren't you going to work?"

"Someone's coming over."

Mom stops exercising and sits up. "Someone's coming over? Now? But you never have people over. I was shocked that Teagan came by."

"Mom, please. Can you just go get dressed?"

"All right, calm down," she says, and gets up. As she's heading upstairs, she says, "What's his name?"

How did she know it was a guy?

"Josh. But he's not . . . it's not a big deal. He's just coming over to hang out."

"Uh huh."

"Mom!"

She says something else but I don't hear it because I've raced into the kitchen, where I call Teagan at work and say I can't pick her up tonight.

"Because of a certain someone?" she says.

"Yep."

"Finally!" she says. "Also, I expect to hear all the details later. Deal?"

"Deal," I say, and then I call Greg. He doesn't answer, of course, so I tell his voice mail that I'm sorry I wasn't in on Saturday and that I'm still so sick I can't get out of bed.

"In fact, I have to go throw up now," I say, and hang up.

"Well, what do you think?" Mom says, and I look over at her.

She's wearing clothes. And not just any clothes, but something approaching true "mom" clothes. Her pants aren't skintight and her shirt actually covers everything and isn't bright pink or red.

"You look . . ." Actually, she looks strange. I'm so used to most of Mom being on display, that having her all covered up is . . . well, it seems wrong, somehow. Like she's not being herself.

"I assume that means I look acceptable," Mom says, smiling. "Now go get ready, and I'll try and shove the worst of the dust under something before Josh gets here. And Hannah, I have to start work by nine at the latest, so you'll either have to have him go home or take him out somewhere, okay?"

Take him out. Have him take me out. Yeah, that would be okay. It would be the most amazing thing ever, actually.

I nod, and then race upstairs to my room, where I spin around in a circle. This is really happening. Josh is coming here. Well, not here. I'm not bringing him up to my room.

I'd like to, though.

I'd really like to.

As I'm getting dressed, I try to think about things that aren't me and Josh in my room. I'm moderately successful, if only because I realize I have nothing to wear. I mean, I have clothes, but for once I sort of want to . . .

I sort of want to show off the fact that I have curves. So I visit Mom's closet, where I try on a short black skirt and matching shirt.

One look in the mirror confirms that I can't wear this outfit. At least, I can't wear it where anyone could see me. I look . . .

I don't look bad or anything. I just look—I didn't realize how much my chest sticks out when I'm wearing a shirt that fits. Also, I haven't shown so much leg since . . . well, ever. The skirt goes back into the closet, and I pull on a pair of my own jeans. The shirt doesn't fall down over the jeans like my shirts do, and there's a little strip of skin showing right below my navel.

I tug the shirt down. It pops back up. I put one of my shirts on over it.

Now I look like me. Straight up and down.

For once, I don't like it. I don't want to look like this. I take the top shirt off, and look at myself in Mom's little black shirt and my jeans.

It's not bad. I think I look okay. Pretty, even. Maybe.

I look at myself in the mirror again, and then I take the ponytail holder out of my hair.

I lean forward and swish my hair around a little bit. I stand back up.

Oh, not good. I brush my hair, and then tuck it behind my ears. Better.

I feel a bit strange dressed like this, though. Like I'm not being me.

Weird. However, I don't have time for an existential crisis now, so I take a deep breath and start to go downstairs.

"Hannah?" Mom says when she sees me. "You look . . . oh, Hannah. You look so much like me."

Before I can figure out if the proper response to that should be "Um, okay," or simply a mad flight to go change, the doorbell rings.

"He's here?" I say. "How can he be here?"

"You've been getting dressed for about an hour," Mom says, and smiles at me. "You go back upstairs. I'll get the door, and then you walk down and let him see you."

"Uh . . ." My brain is still stuck on the fact that he's here.

Mom laughs and steers me toward the stairs. I start to walk up them, and then stop halfway, nervous and happy.

"Hi, Josh," I hear Mom say. "I'm Hannah's mom. We met once before, I think. Anyway, come on in! Hannah's coming down right now."

He's here. He's really here. He's going to see me.

Maybe I can just yell down that I'm sick. Or dying. Or both. I'll just—

"Hannah, Josh is here," Mom says, and then Josh is right in front of me, standing at the foot of the stairs and smiling.

And once I see him smiling like that, nothing matters.

Why?

Because he isn't smiling at me. He isn't even looking at me. He's smiling at Mom.

twenty-eight

You know how sometimes you have a dream that's bad—not scary monsters waiting to eat you bad, but plausible bad, like you stand up in class and forget what you're going to say and everyone laughs?

Now is just like that. Only it's not a dream.

Josh has brought presents. He hands them to me but I'm pretty sure they aren't actually for me. He's given me lilies, listed on Mom's site as her favorite flower, and chocolate-covered mints, just like the ones he gave me before.

Just like Mom likes.

"It's so great to see you again," he says to Mom. "My older brother—he just turned twenty-seven—loved *Cowboy Dad*. When I was little, we used to watch episodes he'd recorded, and I thought you were the most beautiful woman ever."

"Oh, well, thank you," Mom says, glowing like she always does around praise even as her gaze skitters over to me. "I had no idea anyone your age would have even heard of me."

"Are you kidding? Everyone saw that amazing ad you did for Pizza! Pizza! Pie! All the guys in my band love it. We even wrote a song, 'Dream Girl,' about it."

This isn't happening. I look at him. He's still looking at Mom. It's happening.

"Hannah, let me take this stuff," Mom says, and reaches for "my" gifts. "I'm sure you and Josh want to talk. Josh, it was lovely to see you, and I know you and Hannah will—oh, are these mints?"

"They are," Josh says. "The chapter in your autobiography where you talk about sitting on the floor and eating a box of them the day you found out *Cowboy Dad* was canceled—it really got to me."

I bet it did. That and the picture Mom put in of herself in her *Cowboy Dad* outfit right next to it, a color portrait of her smiling and bursting out of her "authentic Western" dress.

"Well, thank you," Mom says. "I can't believe you read the book." She glances at me, then bites her lip and goes into the kitchen.

"Wow, she's amazing," Josh says, and finally looks at me. "I've been dying to meet her—for real, you know—and when you agreed to let me come over—well, thank you. You're so special."

"I—"

"No, you really are," he says, cutting me off, and then he smiles at me and leans in.

Is he going to—?

He is.

He does.

He kisses me.

He actually has the nerve to kiss me.

And I'm actually pathetic enough to want it. I know I'm actually beyond pathetic, but it's Josh and he's so beautiful and he wants to kiss me.

So we kiss.

It's awful.

I can't believe it, but it is. I have pictured kissing Josh at least three times a day since I first started working at BurgerTown, and those kisses have ranged from tentative, gentle lip brushes to full-on make out sessions, the kind that start when he catches up to me as I'm walking out to my truck and just grabs me and kisses me.

I didn't picture his tongue shoving into my mouth and then energetically moving around with no preliminaries at all. It feels like I'm being licked by something in a really intrusive and unpleasant way.

I pull back and say, "Um," but before I can say anything else, Josh is "kissing" me again, even more enthusiastically this time. His tongue is poking at my gums (eww) and it's very wet and I can't believe I ever worried that one kiss was going to turn me into Jackson.

Right now I'm more worried it's going to send me off screaming to a nunnery.

"Okay," I say, moving away. "That's really . . ."

"I know," Josh says, grinning at me. "I knew it would be like this. Peyton's pissed at me, but it's worth it. So, do we get to be in the room while your mom does her show, or do we have to watch on your computer or something?"

"Her show?"

"Yeah," he says, still smiling. "I can't wait. She did this one chat a while ago in an alien outfit, and it was so hot that . . ." He trails off as I back away. "I mean, it was hot in an ironic way, obviously."

"Obviously," I say. He's into my mother. Like, really into her.

"So I'll just call Peyton and tell her I'm going to be here with you tonight, okay?" he says, and pulls out his cell phone.

"Wait," I say. "Does Peyton know that you . . . does she know that you're a . . . fan of my mom's?"

"And you." He tries to touch my face.

I move away. "Right. Does she know?"

He nods. "She didn't get it at first, but this weekend, when you were in New York, we had a long talk and she's okay with it now."

"She knows I went to New York?"

"Yeah. When you didn't come in for work on Saturday, I figured you went. I bet it was amazing."

Well, now I know how everyone found out about the video, and can guess exactly which girl hates me and Mom enough to do it.

I look at Josh, and it's like everything I saw in him is gone and there's just a cute asshole making a phone call to one girl so he can do whatever he thinks he's going to do with me while waiting to see my mother in her underwear.

"You know what?" I say when he's off the phone. "Mom has

a whole bunch of promotional stuff she's done out in the garage. I'm sure she'd love to show it to you."

"Really?"

"Yeah. Go on in the kitchen and ask her," I say. "I'll be there in a couple of minutes. I've just got to call work because I forgot to earlier."

He's already headed for the kitchen before I finish the sentence, and when he's gone I grab my keys and bolt.

I could tell him to go, but the thing is, I'm so shocked by who Josh actually is that I don't want to be around him right now. I just want to get away.

There's an old shirt I wore to work one night and got mustard on in the truck, and I put it on over the stupid top I'm wearing and drive, bundling my hair back into a ponytail at a stoplight.

I imagine Josh dying in lots of horrible ways, but I don't cry. This is the second time I've fallen for a big bunch of lies in what must be a record-setting short amount of time.

I can't believe I thought he liked me.

But I did. Until he got to the house and I saw him smiling at Mom, I thought he . . .

I can't believe the stuff I thought. Soul mate? I'm an idiot.

I drive to work. I know I called in sick, but I could use the money, and . . . I don't know. I'm here. I park the truck, and then I put my head down on the steering wheel and cry. No one can see me here, and now no one will know how stupid I've been. At least I have that.

It's not much, but right now it's all I've got, and I tell myself that over and over again until I stop crying. Then I get out of the truck and go into work.

Greg's in his office, leaning back in his chair staring at the ceiling.

"Hey, sorry about the message I left before," I say. "I thought I was still sick but I'm not, so now I'm here."

"You were sick?" Greg says. "When? You didn't eat any of those fries that were in the break room earlier, right? Because those have been there a long time and BurgerTown can't be held responsible for—"

"No, I meant when I—never mind," I say, and go to the call room. And when I walk in, Finn says, "Hannah? What are you doing here? Josh called and said you two were hanging out."

I take a deep breath. "He . . . it didn't work out," I say, and sit down. "You can send some orders over here in a second. I just have to sign in."

"What happened?" Finn says.

"Nothing."

"Oh. You just seem . . . never mind."

"What?"

"I don't know. Is everything okay?"

"Let's just say Josh thinks my mother is . . . well, let's just say she has a definite fan base in the younger male demographic."

"Really?" Finn laughs, but then stops when he sees my face and turns bright red. "I didn't mean it like that. Hannah, I—"

"Shut up," I say. "One word, one remotely teasing word, and I swear I will jab something painful into your eye. Repeatedly."

So Finn shuts up, and we work.

twenty-nine

Josh doesn't come in at all—he probably doesn't even realize I've left my own house—and when I call home to tell Mom where I am in case she's worried, she whispers, "Why did you leave? I can't get this boy to go home and he's . . ."

"A jerk?"

"Well . . . yes. But I thought you wanted him to come over."

"Well, now I don't."

"Did you leave because he . . . um, because he—?"

"Yes, I know he thinks you're hot, Mom. It's okay. I figured it out about two seconds after he showed up."

"I swear I didn't try to—"

"I know."

"And Hannah, you're so wonderful, and I know—"

"I gotta go," I say, and hang up before she can say anything else. I know Mom didn't and isn't encouraging Josh, but right now I don't need to hear her say how "wonderful" she thinks I am after I had to watch the guy I was dumb enough to like drool all over her.

"Don't," I say to Finn, who is looking at me.

"What?"

"Don't say anything."

"Fine," Finn says. "Feel sorry for yourself over the hinky loser who writes bad songs."

"Hinky?"

"It's a word," Finn says. "Sort of."

"Well, it fits him. And I'm not feeling sorry for myself. It's just that I didn't realize Josh is—"

"An enormous pretentious ass?"

"Yeah," I say. "That."

Finn smiles at me. "Well, now you know. Wanna take a break?"

"What, now?"

"Well, I know it's been insanely busy," he says, and gestures at our terminals, which have gone blank due to inactivity.

"Why is it so slow, anyway?"

"I—well, after Josh called, I set it up so that all the incoming orders would go to room C starting about five minutes ago."

"Why would you . . . ? You were going to leave early!"

"Oh, this from the girl who called in sick to hang out with . . ." Finn trails off. "Anyway, let's go buy out the vending machines. I'm starving, and it'll be at least another thirty minutes before anyone over in C figures out what's going on."

"What were you going to do when they figured out you weren't here?"

"I don't know. Get fired, I guess."

"Why would you do that?"

He shrugs. "I saw salt and vinegar chips out there. You know, they're usually gone after a day, so . . ."

So Finn and I go and buy food. Actually, he ends up buying it because I left the house with my keys and eighty cents in the pocket of my jeans.

"Okay, enough," I say as he hands me a third candy bar. "I can't eat all this."

"So save some for later," he says, and we head back to work.

When I sit down, I automatically look over at Josh's terminal.

"Still thinking about him?" Finn says. "Why?"

I shrug. "I just—why don't you go ahead and go home, okay? I can handle everything." To my horror, my voice cracks a little on the last words.

"Hannah," Finn says, and comes over to me, putting his arms on either side of my chair. "Josh is an idiot, okay? And you . . . do you know what you are?"

"Stupid?"

"Beautiful," he says, his face turning red, and it's just Finn standing there, just Finn, but I can't breathe; there isn't enough air in this room, inside me, and I can't stop looking at him, noticing his face and his eyes and his mouth and the little scar by his left eye and the freckles along his cheekbones, and he's looking right at me, not like he's looking for someone else, but like he's fine with what he sees.

"I—" I say, and he kisses me.

It is nothing like kissing Josh. That's the first thing I think.

It's the only thing I think.

I can't think anything else. I can't think at all. It's all sensation, and those feelings I was worried I had but then realized I didn't after kissing Josh?

I have them.

I have plenty of them.

I have them, and Finn and I end up on the floor, wedged up against a terminal station, metal digging into my back. Finn is pressed against my front and I've hooked my legs around his, pulling us closer, and it's not enough. I want more, I want his skin touching mine, my skin touching his, and—

"Oh, I'm so sending your calls back over."

I look up, and through the curtain of my hair—When did it come out of its ponytail? Why is one of my hands under Finn's shirt? Why are both his hands under mine?—I see a woman from call room C glaring at us.

"This isn't what it looks like, Angie," Finn says, shifting a little, and smacks his head against the bottom of a terminal. "Ow!"

"Oh please," Angie says. "I'm thirty-five. I remember sex, sort of. I'm sending your calls back now, plus mine, because I just remembered I have a family emergency exactly like you said you did."

"I didn't say family emergency," Finn says. "I said there was some family stuff and I had to go to the emergency room."

"Yeah, well, I have some family stuff involving me and a

margarita," Angie says. "You've got about thirty seconds before the orders start coming."

I sit up then, and so does Finn. Angie heads back to room C, and sure enough, our terminals start blinking. And then Angie walks back by, purse and car keys in hand.

Finn looks at me. I look at him. To my surprise, his face turns a deep, painfully bright red, the most embarrassed I've ever seen him look.

"I—" he says, and then stops. And then we just sit there. Him, red-faced, and me realizing shirt number one—the baggy one I'd put on after the disaster with Josh—is shoved up around my shoulders.

It's so quiet. And it probably hasn't been that long since Angie came in, but it feels like forever and it's horrible because clearly he's embarrassed by what happened, but is it because of what happened? Or because someone saw us? Or—?

I don't know.

I do know I can't believe what just happened, but it did, and with Finn.

Finn. I just . . . I don't think of him like that.

Except I clearly do.

I force myself to get up, sit in my chair, and say, "Hi, welcome to BurgerTown, home of the Better Burger, may I take your order?" I don't look at him. I can't.

Actually, I can, but I just don't want him to see me looking. I sneak a peek anyway. His face is still red. What is he thinking?

"Hello? Hello! Did you get my order?" a customer says.

"Of course," I say, and try to pay attention and not think about Finn. Or what just happened. Or how great it felt.

Or how much I wish Angie hadn't come in.

Luckily, it gets busy—the kind of busy I usually hate, with people wanting special orders and details about ingredients, and I don't have a chance to think about Finn or what happened.

Not that much of a chance, anyway, and when the night shift people come in we're still taking orders. I wrap mine up first and bolt for the parking lot. I think I hear Finn say something as I leave the room, but I don't stick around to listen.

thirty

Mom isn't home when I get there, but she's left a
note on my dresser.

"Had to get rid of Josh, so I told him I do the show elsewhere
and just say I'm at home. I'm at the backup site if you need me."

Wow. Mom hates the backup site because it's cramped and
smells like computer guys. Josh must have really driven her crazy.

Good.

The phone rings. I don't bother to answer it, but I do check
and see if there's a message afterward.

There is. It's from Josh.

"I just wanted to thank you for talking to me, Candy," he
says. "I had a wonderful time, and my brother is going to love the
autographed book. I also wanted to let you know that I've been

inspired to write three new songs tonight and it's all thanks to you. Oh, and tell Hannah I can't wait to see her at school."

What an ass. "Tell Hannah I can't wait to see her at school," and he even sounds like he means it. I don't think I could have picked a worse guy to be my soul mate. I can't believe I thought he was my soul mate. I mean, he's charming and he knows how to make you feel special, but he's only interested in what he wants, just like Jackson.

Huh.

And ewww.

I go to bed, but of course I can't sleep. I lie there thinking about Josh. And Mom. And Jackson. And how everything has been so crazy that I hardly know—

All right, I'm not actually thinking about any of them. I'm thinking about Finn. About his freckles, his eyes, his mouth. About how I felt when he looked at me.

About kissing him.

That's what I'm thinking about, and despite my efforts to think about something else, my brain will not listen. It just keeps going back to the kissing.

And how it sounds like someone is throwing rocks at my window.

Josh.

Only Josh would do something as stupidly "romantic" as flinging rocks at my window. A million dollars says he thinks it's Mom's room. I get out of bed, picking up the enormous geode José got for me when I turned nine because back then my favorite color was purple and I liked sparkly things.

I heft it in my hands as I open the window. I think I'll tell Josh he should write a song and call it "Rock of Love" right before I smack him in the head.

I lean out, geode ready—and a pebble hits me in the forehead.

"Ow," I say into the dark. "Should I come outside so you can throw larger stones at me?"

"I hit you?"

"Finn?" What's he doing here?

"Yeah," he says, stepping forward so the light I left on in the kitchen catches his face. "Did I really hit you?"

"No, I said 'ow' for the fun of it. Of course you hit me. What are you doing here?"

"I wanted to talk to you. Wait, what are you holding?"

"A geode."

"Why?"

"I thought you were Josh."

"You thought I was Josh?"

"Well, throwing rocks at windows seems like a—well, it seems like a clichéd thing to do. So I figured it was him."

"And you were going to throw that at him? Cool," Finn says.

"I could throw it at you."

"You could, but I'd rather talk to you."

Oh. He wants to talk to me. That's very . . . I don't know. My insides are all fluttery, though.

"Okay," I say, my voice shaking a little, and wait.

He doesn't say anything. I wait a little more.

"I notice you aren't talking," I finally say.

"Well, as much as I'm sure the people next door who are

pretending they aren't looking at me would like to hear what I have to say, I'd rather say it to just you."

"Oh," I say, and stick my head out the window. Sure enough, Mr. and Mrs. Howard are looking at us out of one of their windows. When they see me, they quickly pretend they're looking at the road and shut their window. "Okay, I guess you can come in."

"Um, Hannah, you have to, you know, open the front door so I can actually come in."

"I thought you were going to—you're standing under my window. Aren't you supposed to climb up here or something?"

"My ladder's at home. Also, you call throwing rocks at your window clichéd?"

"Gee, Finn, let me just run downstairs and let you in right now."

"Come on, Hannah," he says. "I'm sorry about before, okay? And I really do want to talk. Apologize or whatever. So could you please let me in?"

I tuck the geode under one arm. He's sorry. He's sorry we kissed. He even wants to apologize for it. That's a nice thing to do, isn't it?

I can't believe he's sorry.

I'm not.

"Hannah?"

"Fine, I'm coming," I say, and go downstairs to let him in.

When I open the door, Finn is standing there with his hands stuffed in his pockets. Once he sees me, his face slowly starts to turn red.

Oh goody.

"Hey," he finally says.

"Hey," I say, and then we both sort of stand there for a while.

"I thought you wanted to come in," I finally say.

"I do," he says. "It's just . . . well, can I come in enough so you can close the door? Your neighbors are looking at us again."

I peer around him, and see Mrs. Howard watching us out another window. I move aside and he comes in, waving at Mrs. Howard as I shut the door. She doesn't wave back.

"Neighbors," I tell him. "Five years here, and they've never said anything to me other than 'Tell your mother to buy better blinds' and 'Must you park your truck so close to our driveway?'"

"I see tonight you managed to box their cars in real good," he says, grinning, and I shrug.

"You're devious," he says. "I like that." And then he blushes again.

"Why are you doing that?"

"Doing what?" he says, turning even redder.

I shift the geode from under my arm to my hand, tired of how it's digging into my skin. "Look, if you came over here to tell me that the . . . stuff that happened earlier was a mistake or whatever, that's fine. I get it. I agree."

"I don't think—you think it was a mistake?"

"Well, it's not like I said to myself, 'Gee, why don't I go into work and roll around on the floor with Finn?'"

He grins at me, his blush fading a little. "What? You mean you haven't been plotting this for weeks? I figured you finally realized we're meant to be and—"

"Finn, it's late, I'm tired, I've had a shitty couple of days. Just say whatever it is you're going to say and then go so I can sleep."

"Oh," he says. "Okay. I didn't mean—I just—I've wanted to . . ." He blows out a breath. "Could you maybe put the rock down?"

"Finn—"

"Seriously," he says, looking directly at me. "I—I don't usually go around throwing rocks at people's windows. Or saying that I've wanted to kiss you since your first day at work, when you wanted to know why we had three codes for fish sandwiches when we only sold one kind."

"What?" I say, stunned, and drop the geode.

It lands on Finn's foot. He sucks in a breath, makes a face, and then lets out a long—long—string of swear words.

"See?" he says. "This is not—I wanted this to go different. Better. I've thought about kissing you forever and I really didn't want to kiss you and have Angie walk in and blackmail us into doing extra work. I didn't want you to be thinking about Josh. I didn't even want you to like him. But you do, and I really—hold on. I think one of my toes is broken."

"You've thought about kissing me?"

"Yeah," he says, and blushes again. "And okay, I'm pretty sure I do have a broken toe. Do you see blood? Is it running out of my shoe?"

"I barely hit your foot. And I don't like Josh."

"Yeah, now."

"I didn't know he was—I thought he was different." I say. "Special."

"Yeah, I know. He drinks lots of coffee. He writes songs. He—"

"I was wrong, though," I say. "When he was over here, even when he wasn't drooling over my mom, I didn't—it's like I liked the idea of him, not him. And when you and me . . ."

Finn looks at me, and his expression is so intense I feel a little shiver—a nice kind of shiver, *that* kind of shiver—pulse through me. "You and me what?"

"Nothing."

He walks toward me. I move back, bumping into the handrail at the bottom of the stairs. "You were going to say something," he says.

"I wasn't."

"Were."

"Wasn't."

"Hannah," he says, and we are so close again, so close I can see his freckles and reach up and touch his hair. I do, and he closes his eyes and shivers, actually shivers, and the way I felt when he looked at me just now comes back about a hundred times stronger.

"I liked kissing you," I tell him, and his eyes open.

"You did?"

I nod. His eyes widen and now I feel a blush burning across my own face.

He starts to say something.

"Don't," I say, and put a hand over his mouth. His lips are soft and warm under my skin, and I curl my hand away, tuck it down against my side.

"But you were thinking about Josh—"

"Now you're a mind reader?"

"You weren't?"

"Was I supposed to?" I say.

"So you really wanted to kiss me?"

"I already said it, didn't I?"

"You didn't say anything afterward, though."

"You didn't either. And normally nothing can shut you up."

"You're not normal," he says. "I mean—well, you aren't, but what I meant is that I—oh, hell," he says.

And then he kisses me again.

We end up in the kitchen, where he takes off his shoes and we determine that none of his toes are broken in between kisses.

"This has been the strangest night of my life," he says, his breath hot against my ear, and goosebumps prickle my skin.

"Mine too," I say, and turn toward him, pulling him in for another kiss.

"I really like your kitchen," he says with a gasp a little while later. I'm leaning against the counter, arms wrapped around him as he leans into me, his mouth on my neck. "I mean, I really, really like—"

"You talk too much sometimes," I say, a fabulous, explosive drumbeat pounding inside me. Finn's hands are warm and careful on my skin, like I'm something precious.

"Not all the time," he mutters through a kiss, and then catches my laugh with his mouth, pulling me even closer. He smoothes a hand over my hair, eyes closing as I push my hips against his.

"Hannah," he says, so softly, so sweetly, a gentle counterpoint to the stunned "Hannah?" I hear from the other side of the room. Which is strange because I haven't heard anything except us, but now—

"I—um. Hi," Finn says, and I open my eyes to see Mom, dressed in a bright blue negligee, staring at us.

thirty-one

I think Mom might be mad. I can't tell. She stares at me and Finn like she can't believe what she's seeing as we separate, and she blinks at Finn as he fixes his shirt, runs a hand through his hair, and says, "I'm Finn. I just came over to . . ."

My mother raises her eyebrows at him. I didn't know she could still do that.

"To talk," he says, blushing. "To Hannah. About work. And school. And, um, rocks."

I elbow him, but it's too late.

"Rocks?" Mom says, her voice slightly higher than normal.

"Not rocks," I tell her. "He's trying to be funny. And he was just leaving."

"I—right," Finn says. "Just give me a minute."

I glance at him, and he gives me a meaningful look.

"Oh," I say.

"I'm making grilled cheese," Mom says, her voice brittle. "Yes, that's what I'm going to do. In fact, right now I'm going to turn around and get a frying pan, and you two are going to not be standing next to each other when I turn back."

"Hey, I love grilled cheese," Finn says, and then looks at me when I elbow him again. "What?"

"You said you needed to leave, remember?"

"You can stay for a sandwich, Finn, if you want," Mom says, dropping the frying pan onto the stove. It lands with a solid, heavy thud.

"He can't. He—"

"I'd love to," Finn says, and moves out of range of my elbow.

So Mom makes sandwiches, not looking at me or Finn the whole time. I keep checking to see if Finn is looking at her, but every time I do, he's either looking at me or looking at the picture of me Mom's framed and hung on the far wall. José took it when I was seven, and I'm sitting on the front steps of our house in Queens, showing off my missing baby teeth with a huge smile.

"That's you, right?" he asks me.

"Yeah."

"Cute. Not that I, uh, think that little kids are cute. Just that you were cute. I mean, you can see how you turned out to be so . . . oh. Thank you," he says as Mom hands him a sandwich.

After a moment, he looks at me. "Can I get a plate?"

I tear off some paper towels and give them to him. "We don't really do plates here."

"Oh," Finn says. "How come?"

"Because I don't eat much," Mom says, sliding her own sandwich onto a paper towel and sitting down at the kitchen table. There's a little robe that goes over her silky negligee, and she's put it on and buttoned it up to her neck. She'd look mom-like if it wasn't bright blue. Or didn't have feathers around the collar.

"Here," she says, handing me two sandwiches, and then looks at me and then Finn and then me again. "Why don't you two sit down?"

Finn does, his sandwich almost gone. "Are you going to eat both of those?" he asks me.

"Yes," I say, and then give him half a sandwich anyway.

"So, you work with Hannah," Mom says to Finn, who nods. "And you go to school with her?"

Finn nods again, and finishes inhaling the half of the sandwich I gave him. "Since ninth grade. That's when I moved here. Well, not just me. Me and my family. My dad got a job teaching French at the community college, and my mom works for Dr. Thomas, the dentist over on 3rd Street. You don't go to him, do you? You shouldn't, because he makes everybody wait forever. My mom says she spends most of the time telling people she's sorry they have to wait so long." He blushes. "That's probably more than you wanted to know. I talk a lot sometimes."

I snort. He grins at me, and bumps one foot against mine under the table, only instead of moving it away like he usually does, he just leaves it there.

It feels nice.

Well, better than nice. It makes me think about what we were doing before Mom came in.

"Well, it's good to meet you," Mom says. "Hannah doesn't have many people over. But it's late, so you should probably go home."

Okay, who is this woman? She looks like my mother, but she's making food and telling people they should go home in a distinctly mother-type way.

"Oh. Right," Finn says. "I was just hoping to talk to Hannah really fast about—"

"I think you've done enough talking for one night," Mom says—snaps, actually—and then smiles. "I mean, it's late, and I'm tired, and I'm sure your parents are wondering where you are."

"Oh no, they always fall asleep before I get home. I could stay out all night if I wanted—um. I'll just get my shoes," Finn says, and gets up.

I walk with him to the front door, Mom a silent bright blue presence behind us. And I think she's actually glowering.

"Okay, I'd better go," he says, lingering by the door, and I can tell he wants one more kiss.

Well, actually, I can't tell. I do know, however, that I want one more, and say, "I'll walk you out to your—"

"No, you should let Finn get home," Mom says. "I'm sure he's tired."

"Actually, I—" Finn says, and breaks off as Mom takes a step forward. "Right. I am pretty tired, actually." He glances at me. "See you later?"

"Sure." I hate that phrase because you never know what it

means. "See you later" can mean anything, or nothing, because who knows what later really is?

"Tomorrow," he says, like he knows what I'm thinking, and then looks at Mom. "Can I talk to you for a second?"

Mom blinks at him, and then the two of them step out onto the porch. He smiles at me, and then pulls the door firmly closed.

I can't hear anything—and I'm listening as hard as I can—but when Mom comes back in she looks . . . I don't know. Sad, and lost, and a little bit like she's going to cry.

"Mom?" I say. "Are you okay?"

She nods.

"What were you two doing out there?"

"Talking."

Grrr. This is like pulling teeth. "About what?"

She looks at me like I'm crazy. "You, Hannah."

"Oh," I say, and when she doesn't respond, add, "And?"

"Well, I . . . okay," Mom says. "He started to say something, but I told him I wanted to know why he thought it was acceptable to come into someone's house and make out with that someone's 17-year-old daughter when no one was home."

"You're kidding, right?" I say as she heads for the living room. "You're . . . what are you here? Angry? Sad? I don't get it. We've had the sex talk and—well, let's face it, I've seen stuff. I mean, hello, Jackson."

"Tonight's just been . . . Hannah, you bring a guy home for the first time ever this afternoon, and then you leave, and leave him here. Then I go to work—to get away from that guy, I might add—and come home to find you with another guy. Can you see how this might be a little confusing for me? You haven't mentioned liking anyone ever, and suddenly you're bringing one guy home and then tongue wrestling—"

"Tongue wrestling?"

She sighs. "I don't know what I'm supposed to say here, Hannah. I always thought that when you showed an interest in sex, it wouldn't bother me. But you're so—you're so young, honey. And if I hadn't come home when I did, I think you and Finn might have—"

"Oh, you so don't get to do this," I say. "You don't think I know how to be responsible? Really? Please."

"I do think you're responsible, but I also think . . ." Mom says, and then sinks onto the sofa. "I just . . . what about the boy from before?"

"You mean Josh, the one who liked you? Is that what this is about? Are you mad that Finn didn't stare at you when he was here?"

"No," Mom says, sounding shocked and hurt. "I don't—you know this is how I dress for—"

"Yeah, I know it's for work. But it's not like you're putting on the layers when you go out. But then, I guess that's free advertising, right?"

"So you are mad," she says. "Hannah, I'm sorry Josh was—well, I don't know what you thought he was. But I promise I didn't encourage him, and if everything with Finn was because of that, I want you to really think about what happened, because trying to get back at me by—"

"Wait, you think what happened with Finn is about you?" I

say. "Oh, I get it. Of course it is, because Candy Madison, minor web star, must be the reason everything happens. She must be the person everyone wants."

"I didn't say—"

"Mom, stop. I'm not mad at you about Josh. I'm not even mad at Josh. And what happened with Finn had nothing to with Josh. Or even—and I know this will be a surprise—you. It just . . . happened."

"Sex doesn't just happen," Mom says. "And people who say it does—"

"First, we didn't have sex, and second, have you heard your-self talk about meeting Jackson?" I say, and then mimic her. "'I saw him, and I was swept away . . .'"

"That's not the same thing."

"How's that?"

She throws her hands up in the air. "Okay, fine. I've done some stupid things in my time. A lot of them. And I don't want—I want better than that for you, and everything that's happened in the past few days has been so difficult that I'm afraid you might make a choice you'll regret. I've done things like that in the past, and I—"

"Yeah, but here's the thing," I say. "I'm not you. I don't—I did like Josh, you're right. But I didn't know him. I just saw him at work and school and I thought...I thought he was the perfect guy. The opposite of Jackson. But he wasn't. And when I figured that out, I left. I shouldn't have stuck you with him, but I did. And I'm sorry about that. But I'm not sorry about anything else."

"Hannah—"

"Wait," I say. "I'm not done. I'm not you, and I'm not Jackson either. I can finally—I can finally see that now. You know, Teagan says I'm scared, and I keep telling her I'm not, but maybe—"

"Wait, Teagan says you're scared? Of what?"

"Me," I say, sitting down next to her. "Finn. The idea of being with someone who's real, who I actually know. Who knows me." And as soon as I say it, it feels right. No, more than that. It feels true.

"You didn't seem scared when I came home and found you in the kitchen. And maybe you should be. You don't want to end up—"

"Sitting around in my underwear acting like people I've never met are the most interesting and attractive people I know?"

"No," Mom says, her voice very soft. "I like my job. I know you don't get that, but I do. What I mean is I don't want you to—I don't want you to end up alone. I'm not sorry I had you, and I hope you know that. But more than anything else, I'm sorry I ever—"

"I know, met Jackson."

"No," she says. "José."

"José?" I say, shocked. "But you and him—you two—"

"Yes," she said. "We loved each other. Jackson loved the idea of me, but José . . ." She looks at the floor. "José really looked at me. Really saw me. Really loved me. And I loved him."

She looks at me. "I loved him, and we were going to be together forever. And then he was gone and I—" She tugs at the bottom of her robe. "Love hurts. It's—love isn't wonderful or magical or any of those things. It's like losing a part of yourself and you can't ever—" She blinks once, twice, and then bites her lip so hard I can see marks left by her teeth. "You can't get it back. José's been gone for years and I'm still—I'm still not whole. He took part of me with him, and I don't want that for you."

She moves in closer, so close I can see that even all the cosmetic injections she's had haven't completely erased the tiny lines around her eyes, the small sad folds by her mouth. "I want you to keep your heart safe. You've always—you've always been so smart about that. You've always been so strong, and I want you to stay like that. I want you to stay safe."

"So, it's not sex that bothers you," I say. "It's . . . you don't want me to like anyone?"

"No, no," she says. "Like people, Hannah. Just don't—just be careful. Don't ever forget that it can all end." Her mouth is shaking and I understand what she's saying. I've always believed it. I've never wanted to be like Mom, never wanted to be some rich old man's play toy or, worse, care about a guy enough that losing him would matter to me.

But now that she's said it out loud, it seems so . . . it seems so sad. So lonely.

So scared.

I take a deep breath. "Are you really sorry?"

"About you? Hannah, no, I've never ever been sorry I had—"

"No," I say. "About José. Are you really sorry you met him? That you loved him?"

She's silent for a long time.

"No," she finally says, her voice so soft, barely a whisper, and then says it again, louder, surprise in her voice. "No. I'm not sorry I met José. I'm not sorry I fell in love with him and that we got married. I know we ended up here because of it, but I wouldn't take back anything because I—"

"Because you loved him," I say.

"I love him," she says. "Not past tense. Not gone. I won't ever love anyone else. Oh, I know that's not how things are supposed to work. I know we were only together a few years, but I know how I feel. How I'll always feel." She shakes her head. "Listen to me. Here I am going on and on and you're making me feel better when I'm supposed to be talking to you about your love life—"

"Mom, don't call it that, please."

She fiddles with her robe hem again. "Finn did say something to me before. He . . . well, he said you need to have your truck engine looked at, that it sounds like there's something wrong with your gears or something."

"The belts," I say. "He told me that too."

"And he—he said he likes you," she says, leaning against me. "It was very sweet, actually. He's—"

"I know," I say. "He's real."

thirty-two

Mom's already up when I drag myself out of bed in the morning, doing exercises on the floor of her room. With her hair pulled back, and wearing yoga pants and a tank top that actually covers her belly button, she looks younger than usual.

She makes a face when I say that. "There's no point in doing all of this—" she says, gesturing at her stomach, "if I'm going to wander around with everything covered up. I work hard to look good, and other people should appreciate it."

She's grinning as she says the last bit. Or grimacing from all the exercise. I can't tell. My eyes are still gritty with sleep. I rub them and ask the one last question I need an answer to.

"Do you ever want Jackson to call you?"

She stops exercising and looks at me. "Sometimes," she says, her voice soft. "He was always able to make me feel like I . . . He was the first man who ever made me feel beautiful. Special." She sits all the way up, wrapping her arms around her knees. "Do you want me to call him? I'm sure if I talked to Fran, she could—"

"No," I say. "I just . . . I was just wondering if you ever want to talk to him even though you know he doesn't—can't—really mean what he says."

"Fran would make sure he called you."

"Yeah, but I don't want Fran to make him call me," I tell her. "I want . . ."

"He'll call," she says. "He won't—he won't apologize, but he will call one day."

"Maybe," I say, and it hurts to say that, but it's true.

She looks at me. "You're right. Maybe he will. I'm sorry. And Hannah, you do know I love—"

"I know," I say. "I love you too."

When I get dressed, I look at the elastic ponytail holder in my hand, and then at my hair. I try to picture myself walking into school with it down. I'd walk down the hall and see Finn and he'd . . .

He'd probably ask me what was wrong. And then he'd grin at me and say . . .

He'd grin at me and say . . .

I don't know. What would he say?

What will he say to me today?

"I knew it!" Teagan says when she answers the phone and I tell her about what happened with Josh and then with Finn at work and ask for advice. "I knew you'd end up with Finn."

211

"You did not! Yesterday you said that you knew I couldn't pick you up because—"

"Of a certain someone," she says. "You just assumed I meant Josh, but I knew it would be Finn. It was totally obvious from the way you talk about him."

"No way, you didn't know . . . Did you really know?"

"Yep," she says. "You like Finn."

"I . . . yeah, I do," I say, and then tell her everything else about last night.

"Tell me the rock part again," she says when I'm done.

"The rock part? He and I end up getting caught by my mother, who goes all mom-like on me, and you want me to tell you about the rocks again?"

"Do you know how many people have guys coming over and throwing rocks at their window so they can talk about how they feel? One. You. You are it in the whole wide world, Hannah. I bet it was way more romantic than you made it sound, too."

"Yeah, having my mother go all mom-like was hot."

"Oh, just admit it already," she says. "You like him. He likes you. You have a whole romance thing going on."

"Fine. We're going to run away and live happily ever after and you can come stay with us in our big stone castle—oh, wait, Jackson has one of those and his life isn't a fairy tale for anyone in it except him."

"Listen to you," she says. "You don't know exactly what's going to happen when you see him and it's making you crazy. Well, crazier than usual. You're just going to have to trust that when he said he likes you he meant it and—"

"Quit being all . . . you," I say, laughing, and then add, "Do you think he meant it?" in a rush.

"Yes," she says. "So you go up to him when you see him and smile and then—"

"Go up to him? I don't go up to people and start talking. You know that."

"He came over to talk to you, right?" When I don't say anything, she says, "You know I'm right. So go on and finally put everything out there, Hannah."

"Okay, I will. But you have to find three schools you want to go to and start applying."

"Hannah—"

"No, I'll talk to Finn, and then tonight you can tell me about the schools, and when you get out of Slaterville I'll come visit and—"

"I'm not doing it," she says.

"You are too. You still have your sketchbook and it's not like you've forgotten how to sew. I mean, you're still making clothes, so—"

"You don't get it. It's not going to happen, okay? I'm not doing it. I don't want to do it. I don't want to—I don't want to fail again."

"Teagan—"

"Don't be scared about Finn," she says. "Take a chance and try being happy, okay? Then you can tell me what it's like."

"But—"

"I'll talk to you later," she says, and hangs up.

This isn't how things are supposed to go. Teagan is supposed to get out of Slaterville. She's supposed to go back to school. She's not supposed to—

She's not supposed to be scared too. But she is. I finish pulling my hair back and go to school.

I don't talk to Finn when I get there. In fact, I don't talk to anyone when I get there. I spent so long talking to Mom and then Teagan that I end up getting to school after the late bell for first period has already rung.

Michelle's in the office when I go to get a tardy slip, talking to the secretary. "I know this is the third time I've been late this term, but I can't help it," she says. "My dad's renovating our house and my sister and I have to share a bathroom. It's like living in the dark ages or something."

"That's not much of an excuse," the secretary says.

"Which is why you know it can't possibly be a lie," Michelle says, and the secretary shakes her head, grinning.

"How much younger is she?"

"Two years."

"Mine's a year and a half," the secretary says, and hands Michelle a late pass with a smile. "Try getting up before she does. That's what worked for me."

"Thanks," Michelle says. "Hey, can Hannah get a pass too? She drove me here and then she had to find a place to park, so it's not her fault she's late. She had to wait for me."

The secretary sighs, but gives me a late pass as well.

"Sister?" I ask Michelle when we're out in the hall. "Since when do you have a sister?"

"Since I can't afford to get any more tardy slips," Michelle says with a grin. "See you later?"

Normally I'd just nod and walk away. I wouldn't even think about what she's said. But I think about it now, and let myself believe she means it. That she really does want to see me later.

"Sure," I say, and when she waves at me before she heads to class, I wave back.

I see Josh in the hall before second period, holding hands with Peyton as a cluster of people, mostly girls, walk with them. He's carrying his notebook, its cover tattered just enough so everyone can see there's lots of writing underneath, and he's talking really loudly about how our generation doesn't know how to feel things. He sees me, smiles, and says, "Thanks for last night, Hannah. It was amazing."

Peyton's smile dims and she glares at me. All the girls around him are looking at me, half with wishes written all over their faces, the other half with a mix of sadness and anger.

Josh is just a guy. And not even a very nice one. I can't believe I didn't see it.

I didn't want to see it. I didn't think he'd ever really notice me, and in the end, he didn't.

And now? Well, now I think—no, I know—I deserve better.

"I'm sorry I had to leave right after you came over but, well, work's more important than you," I say. "Oh, and my mom says if you want to come over again and talk about how much you like her old TV show and stuff, you should call first, because she's really pretty busy. And she also said to tell you it's nice that 'Dream Girl' is about her, but it's the sixteenth or eighteenth song that's been written for her and so she's not interested in hearing it."

The girls with faces full of wishes looked surprised. Some of the angry-looking ones grin. Peyton looks puzzled, and then says, "You said 'Dream Girl' was about me."

"I—" Josh says, and I walk away. I don't need to hear what he has to say. I don't want to hear it. I'm sure I'll hear all about his version of it at work anyway.

Maybe I'll stop along the way and buy some earplugs.

And then I see Finn. He's standing outside the door of my class, hands in his pockets and shrugging at something Brent says. As I watch, he turns and somehow manages to knock a soda out of the hand of the guy standing next to him.

The soda lands on Brent, who stomps past me, swearing and making a face at his soaked shirt. He also has a black eye.

I walk over to Finn. "You do that stuff on purpose," I say.

Finn shrugs. "Brent was the only person who talked to me when I first moved here, and sometimes he's still that guy, but other times . . . well, other times he needs a soda spilled on him."

"Or get pushed into a locker? Or get a black eye?"

"Yeah," he says, and smiles at me.

I wish I'd noticed how sweet his smile was before. I wish I'd really seen it. But at least I see it now.

"Hey, I, uh—here," he says, and pulls a folded piece of paper out of his pocket.

I open it. It says that Hannah James owns Star 4356473, and has a little map of how to find it in the night sky.

"You bought me a star?"

He blushes. "Remember when you said—?"

"I remember. I didn't think you did. I didn't think you'd—I

can't believe you did this." I trace the star's location with one finger. "Thank you."

He shrugs, but he's still blushing. "I was thinking—"

A teacher passing by says, "Class attendance isn't optional, you know," and Finn says, "Yeah, okay," and turns around, ready to walk away.

"Hey," I say, and he stops and faces me. "Would you—maybe sometime we could look for my star or something."

"Yeah?" he says, and I take a deep breath.

"I'd like to," I say, and, in the end, it's not hard to talk to someone I like. Not when Finn is smiling at me like he is now.

"I told you we were meant to be," he says, still smiling, still so Finn, who was always here but who I just didn't see, and now—

Well, now I kiss him.

And just for the record, it's totally worth the tardy slip I end up getting.

ABOUT THE AUTHOR

Elizabeth Scott grew up in a town so small it didn't even have a post office, though it did boast an impressive cattle population. She's sold hardware, pantyhose, and had a memorable three-day stint in the dot-com industry, where she learned that she really didn't want a career burning CDs. She is also the author of *Bloom*, *Perfect You*, *Stealing Heaven*, and *Living Dead Girl*. She lives just outside Washington, DC, with her husband; firmly believes you can never own too many books; and would love it if you visited her website, located at www.elizabethwrites.com.